CHRONICLES

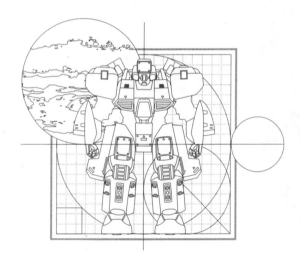

TABLE OF CONTENTS

▶ DREAM POD 9

▼ WRITING

Stuart Elle — Writer

Jason M. Robertson — Additional Writing

Marc A. Vézina — Senior Editor/ Developer

Hilary Doda — Copy Editor

▼ PRODUCTION

Pierre Ouellette — Art Direction/ Designer

Jean-François Fortier — Layout Artist

Ghislain Barbe — Illustrator/Colorist

Patrick Boutin Gagné — Illustrator

Marc Ouellette — Computer Illustrator/Colorist

John Wu — Illustrator/Colorist

▼ ADMINISTRATION

Robert Dubois — Administration

▼ SILHOUETTE

Gene Marcil — System Designer

Stephane I. Matis — System Designer

Marc A. Vézina — System Developer

▼ SPECIAL THANKS

Christian Schaller

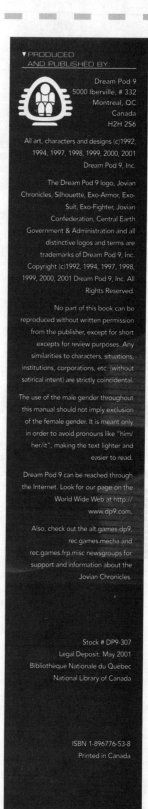

▼ PRODUCED
AND PUBLISHED BY:

Dream Pod 9
5000 Iberville, # 332
Montreal, QC
Canada
H2H 2S6

All art, characters and designs (c)1992,
1994, 1997, 1998, 1999, 2000, 2001
Dream Pod 9, Inc.

The Dream Pod 9 logo, Jovian
Chronicles, Silhouette, Exo-Armor, Exo-
Suit, Exo-Fighter, Jovian
Confederation, Central Earth
Government & Administration and all
distinctive logos and terms are
trademarks of Dream Pod 9, Inc.
Copyright (c)1992, 1994, 1997, 1998,
1999, 2000, 2001 Dream Pod 9, Inc. All
Rights Reserved.

Dream Pod 9 can be reached through
the Internet. Look for our page on the
World Wide Web at http://
www.dp9.com.

Also, check out the alt.games.dp9,
rec.games.mecha and
rec.games.frp.misc newsgroups for
support and information about the
Jovian Chronicles.

Stock # DP9-307
Legal Deposit: May 2001
Bibliothèque Nationale du Québec
National Library of Canada

ISBN 1-896776-53-8
Printed in Canada

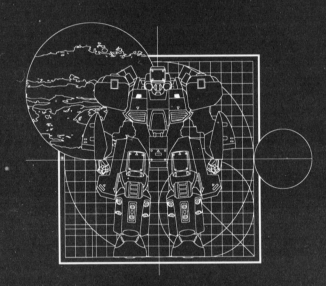

"I live here because I can. It's the same attitude that brought my ancestors into space. No complaints. No regrets. Just survival and prosperity. It's an attitude that's worked for each successive generation, so why stop now?"

— Raymond Troppmann, Explorer/Prospector/Scientist

WELCOME TO THE SPACER'S GUIDE ◄

The quote on the preceding page characterize some of the aspects of life beyond Earth's atmosphere within the Solar System. While the daily struggle for survival on the frontiers of human existence still occupies some people, many more are living in the more "civilized" regions of the Solar System — the settlers following the pioneers. The **Jovian Chronicles Spacer's Guide** is a reference book for daily living in the **Jovian Chronicles** universe. This game supplement explores the small things in life, such as food, clothes, bills and leisure. It describes aspects of commerce, travel and the places people live. Earth, though part of the **Jovian Chronicles** universe, is not covered here, since the subject of life on Earth has been covered in the **Earth Sourcebook** and **In the Shadow of CEGA**.

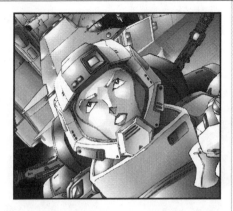

BOOK CONTENT ▼

The **Spacer's Guide** contains five sections in addition to this introduction. Each has a specific focus that introduces Players to different aspects of life in the 23rd century. The level of detail presented in each chapter varies depending on the subject; the intent is to provide specifics about the more mundane and common aspects of life in the Solar System, while leaving more of the larger aspects of daily life to the imagination of Players and Gamemasters.

Living in Space introduces Players and GMs to life on and around the planets in the 23rd century. The chapter begins with a description of the places in which people live, followed with sections on the cost of living and common expenses such as food and drink, clothing, travel and emergencies. All of these sections provide the reader with an expanded understanding of life in space, and a sampling of the details of space-borne life.

Traveling in Space describes how the civilian population travels the Solar System. Passenger travel information includes passenger services, fares and descriptions of each part of the trip, from arrival to departure. Typical cargo rates and customs inspections are also described. The chapter includes a primer on basic space navigation principles and the regulations that govern travel between the planets.

Working in Space details some of the jobs specific to a civilization that lives in space. It covers the many financial and trade aspects of civilian life and offers a look at the activities the crew undertakes to operate a spacefaring vessel. The chapter also covers the use of spacesuits, airlocks and M-pods. Sections on construction and salvage close the chapter with information about both the new and the old in creating structures and vessels.

Playing in Space brings a whole new dimension to having fun in the 23rd century. While many normal gravity sports are still enjoyed, sports adapted to low gravity and microgravity are also common where these conditions exist. The chapter covers more than sports, with a whole range of popular pastimes described or mentioned.

The final chapter covers various game resources for Players and Gamemasters alike. The main section gives Players their first glimpse at the Spacer's Runic language, with a brief primer on its basic syntax and use. The second section describes seven new character archetypes — with several variations of each — based on the topics in this sourcebook. Finally, important excerpts from one of the main 23rd century's space treaties is included, along with a basic glossary of space-related terms.

HOOKS AND TIPS ▯

There are lots of ideas to be had. Much of the information presented is a canvas that the Players and Gamemaster stand their characters and story in front of. Some of the information is about things that would exist in a character's knowledge and thinking as they exist in the **Jovian Chronicles** universe. Undoubtedly, Players and Gamemasters will have their own vision of their game universe, so feel free to use this sourcebook as is, or adapt it to fit the group's vision.

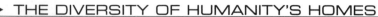

INTRODUCTION

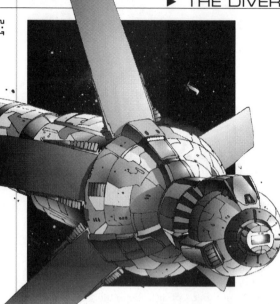

▶ THE DIVERSITY OF HUMANITY'S HOMES

Human civilization has spread across the Solar System, extending out as far as the orbit of Saturn. In each new and dangerous environment, Humankind has had to adapt and create new ways of living, working and thriving. Even though the inhabitants of Earth often lump space-dwellers into a single, homogeneous group with a single lifestyle, creed and set of customs, the truth is far different.

Nothing conforms entirely to its stereotypes, and Humanity's space settlements are no exception. Playing against expectations can be a powerful tool for GMs seeking to impress upon Players the precise nature of their new environment. Not only that, but it helps to bring a sense of realistic diversity to the backdrop. For this reason GMs should consider giving a settlement a characteristic or two that seems directly opposed to the nature of space-based living in general. Joshua's Station, a Jovian colony cylinder, is just such a case. The chaos of that facility directly subverts the general expectation of well-ordered colony cylinders, and the effect is stronger for it.

▼ COLONY CYLINDERS

Colony cylinders are the single most recognizable symbol of Humanity's conquest of space. While there are many kinds of colony cylinders, encompassing a bewildering array of shapes and sizes, all are organized along similar principles. Colony cylinders all enclose a vast, pressurized volume within a shell of spinning metal and rock. The interior surface of this volume becomes a tremendous area of habitable land. In the O'Neill configuration only fifty percent of this area can be used for human habitation, the other half being occupied by the giant windows used to illuminate the interior. Vivarium cylinders, on the other hand, use a powerful lighting system, called a sunline, that runs the length of the cylinder along the rotational axis; this doubles their habitable surface area for the same basic geometry.

Both Vivarium- and O'Neill-type cylinders attract and generate remarkably unified populations. Colony cylinders are at once the most comfortable and yet blatantly artificial of spaceborne human dwellings. One cannot live in a colony cylinder and not know, simply by looking up at the sky to where the ground wraps back around, that one is living in an immense container. From this simple observation comes a very easy way of defining who is part of one's community: all those who live in the same cylinder. The same obervation cannot be easily made with asteroid communities, though, and with planets it is too vast a set to be meaningful. For those who make their home in space inside a colony cylinder, it is most obvious: combined with the close quarters, a sense of community inevitably emerges. Colony cylinders of all types bear a firm kinship to the archetypal society of industrialized Humanity — the city.

One further difference separates those living in colony cylinders and in other environments: by the standards of space, colony cylinders are remarkably benign. Little specialized knowledge is needed to survive in a colony cylinder (although, more likely that not, such knowledge is required to make a living on one). Artistic endeavors are not a desperate delaying measure against the onset of monotony, as they are for those living on asteroids, but a matter of luxury and social grace. The denizens of colony cylinders are typically very quiet and reserved in their individual pursuits and entertainment, however; an audio player with headphones are virtually the only audio equipment a colony-dweller is likely to own.

The environment often overwhelms those new to colony cylinders; it is no small feat to learn to live with the world wrapped around the sky. The phenomenon is worse yet in O'Neill cylinders, where planets and ships can be seen spinning past. Usually people board a colony cylinder by way of a dock located on the axis at the end of the cylinder. On occasion, a system of shuttles that depart and arrive tangentially from the cylinder skin is used as an alternative. In either case, the newcomer will soon be introduced to the well-developed public transportation network that is mandatory in all colony cylinders. The buildings of the cylinder will also seem remarkably small to the newcomer, particularly compared to the shockingly large structure of the cylinder itself. Mild weather can also be expected on a cylinder. The larger the cylinder, the more varied the weather can become, but it is never allowed to become strong enough to cause damage.

OTHER INSTALLATIONS ▼

While colony cylinders are the premier expression of human survival independent of natural bodies, there are many people who still live in smaller facilities. The primary difference is the lack of a large pressurized volume. As a result, the environment is much less world-like. Most of these smaller outposts rotate, or at least have a rotating section, to allow for long-term habitation. Life on these stations is usually dominated by the particular reason for its existence. Commercial and military applications often require such small and relatively isolated outposts. Even when the purpose of a station is military, it usually has a significant number of civilian personnel aboard to provide for the needs of the military installation. The civilians often outnumber the military personnel and may stay much longer than all but the most senior officers before moving on to a more permanent home. In the vast majority of these cases, the commanding officer of the station is also granted the title of military governor, providing him with authority over most civil functions.

Stations with a commercial purpose show greater variation. Some are bustling trading posts whereas others thrive on secrecy, conducting elusive investigations at the borders of the Edicts and beyond. More common are smaller outposts that serve specific needs: cargo-handling stations around Jupiter, satellite repair stations in orbit of Mars and terraforming observation stations above Venus. Life aboard any of these stations is controlled mostly by two factors: the culture of which the station is an offshoot, and the physical nature of the station itself. In general, these smaller stations have to deal with some of the same technical issues encountered by Nomads in the Belt, but they usually also have a much larger and closer industrial base from which to draw upon to solve these issues. While technical aptitude is prized for the citizens, it is not so crucial to be entirely self-reliant since help is never far away.

GHOSTS ★

Ghosts are the people who fall between the cracks of social programs or become alienated with the "system," living desperate lives in an habitat where poverty is a rare case. The most common example is the scrounger who lives discreetly among the various pipe systems beneath the streets of a colony cylinder, or among the machinery of a space station. Ghosts are rarities, with no more than two dozen at most in the largest colony cylinders. Refer to the Ghost archetype on page 70 for more information about these enigmatic characters.

HOOKS AND TIPS

SPACE STATION EXAMPLES ⟐

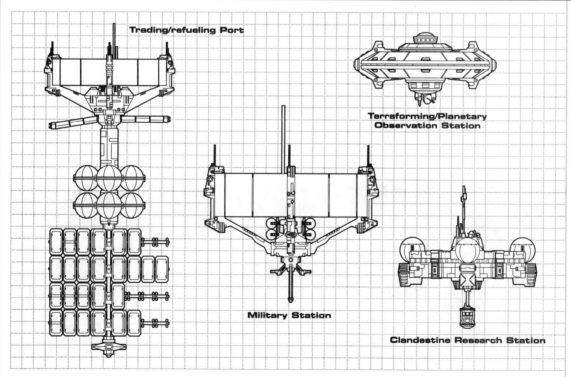

Trading/refueling Port

Terraforming/Planetary Observation Station

Military Station

Clandestine Research Station

INTRODUCTION

▼ ASTEROIDS

Asteroids are among the most technically challenging of all the environments that humans have colonized. One massive terraforming solution does not fit all; rather, a series of unique challenges is discovered, and most often met, with each new rock. The vast majority of asteroids — and many of all colonized asteroids — are found in the main Belt between Jupiter and Mars. For the most part, the inhabitants of these asteroids are Nomads, though each Solar nation maintains a few asteroid habitats under its own flag for research, reconnaissance and military logistical support purposes. Even those habitats, however, usually rely heavily on the expertise gathered by decades of Nomads.

Most asteroids are irregularly shaped and possessed of little gravity. When these rocks are colonized they are almost universally equipped with a gravity wheel for medical reasons. While long-term asteroid dwellers may not think they have need of the dense bones and strong heart muscles of their dirt-bound ancestors, a great deal of biomedical expertise disagrees with them. Each asteroid that is equipped with a gravity wheel requires a unique engineering solution. Save in the cases of the very largest asteroids, the unbalanced torque of a gravity wheel would eventually present complications to maintaining the asteroid's stability. Accordingly, such gravity wheels are installed with one or more flywheels to maintain a zero-torque status for the ensemble. In some cases, such arrangements are slightly modified to de-spin a slowly rotating asteroid, or even to turn an asteroid to a position where the rotation and Solar revolution are in resonance; in such situations, thermal loads can become unbalanced, requiring additional measures. Sometimes, a particular rock may prove unsuited for a gravity wheel or even a simple centrifuge. In such case, the inhabitants are condemned to a largely losing battle waged with exercise and drugs against the threats of calcium loss and muscular atrophy. Few, if any, of those native to these asteroids will ever be able to set foot on a planet.

It is rare for a gravity wheel to take up the majority of the habitable volume of a colonized asteroid. The mechanical stresses and maintenance requirements of such wheels tend to keep the designs as small as possible. People live and work in microgravity conditions, either inside the asteroid itself or in pressurized structures constructed on its surface. When asteroids were first inhabited, it was primarily for commercial gain, with teams of specialized and extraordinarily over-educated miners spending shifts measured in years on a single asteroid before returning to their homes on Earth. With the days of interplanetary commerce only now returning, the majority of those living on asteroids are doing so as a part of the clan-based Nomad lifestyle, and no longer for short-term financial gain.

Asteroids are challenging environments for visitors. While some of the more trade-oriented outposts may have areas optimized for outsiders, the majority of asteroids consist of ad hoc warrens with little overall rhyme or reason to guide the uninitiated. A Nomad is likely to show little sympathy to a clumsy visitor, and tourist ignorance will likely be seen as a danger to the Nomad and to his clan.

The larger inhabited asteroids sometimes bear more resemblance to the comfortable interior of a Vivarium cylinder than to their lesser brethren. Often, one or more large caverns have been hollowed out, allowing a truly massive shirtsleeve environment. These asteroids also boast well-developed transportation networks. Such networks cannot usually be truly called "public," for they typically charge those who are not members of the main resident clan (or the clan which build it). The most typical system is a micro-monorail network in which small passenger cars travel along a groove set into the floor of a corridor. The groove itself is inlaid with a superconducting power conduit.

INHOSPITABLE PLANETS ▼

Before Humanity truly began to explore and exploit space, there was considerable debate as to what the appropriate targets of human colonization should be. Attention focused on orbital habitats, Earth's Moon and Mars. The great surprise of history after the Fall was how successful all these models, once thought of as competing, turned out to be. Necessity was the mother of invention, and out of the hardships came the diversified civilizations of the twenty-third century. The debate that had formed over the axis of contention between the Moon, Mars and space had overlooked the path the truth would take. Mercury and Venus, where even basic exploration was once thought to be impossible, both became targets for significant habitation. Titan, while always intriguing, seemed too far away to be practical, until the growing demand for hydrocarbons made its exploitation inevitable. Mars has changed more in less time than virtually any terraformer could have imagined. Of all the inhospitable celestial orbs, only the Moon has remained much as it was envisioned by Humanity's early dreams.

1.2.4

MERCURY ◇

The most precarious foothold of Humanity lies on Mercury, where skilled technicians lie buried beneath the crust for months, awaiting darkness so that they may attend to the power-collection machines that they serve. No other environment offers so much claustrophobia, and so little hope for release. There is never an opportunity for an unscheduled EVA, and the cameras trained outside show only the swollen sun and the seared landscape of Mercury itself. Psychological stability is a premium among those serving time on the surface of the planet. Great resources are expended in making that experience less traumatic, a task made easier by the availability of almost limitless amounts of solar power.

Very few people are disappointed when the long day is over, and they can begin their surface chores alongside the relief crew from the orbital stations in Mercury's shadow. It is on those stations that Mercurian civilization truly thrives. Much like the Jovian Vivarium cylinders in basic construction, they are far fewer in number. While Jovian wealth comes from the near-effortless supply of their gas-mining skyhooks, every Mercurian is intimately familiar with the source of the power to support their existence under the harshest brunt of the sun, and they think of themselves as a much harder and more pragmatic people for it.

TUNNELS ★

While mining is no longer the primary industry conducted beneath the surface of Mercury, there are still kilometers of old tunnels that go unused by the continuing development of solar collector system. Some of the these old tunnels are used for contingency stockpiles. (What those contingencies are is subject to considerable latitude.) Some tunnels are being used for hydroponics, though the small water supply is a major hindrance to developing the system sufficiently to fully supply the colony cylinders above.

One thing is for certain, the Mercurians are fiercely protective of the planet that shades them from the sun and provides them with power. The Mercurians will not allow any foreign vessel unsupervised access to the planet's surface. Their concern is that someone will establish a covert base of operations in a section of the abandoned mine tunnels. To this end they have collapsed any entrance they are not using themselves, and they constantly monitor all local space traffic to ensure no vessel tries to land. During surface maintenance operations, all personnel and vehicles are closely monitored to ensure that nothing beyond the required surface activities occurs.

SCIENTIFIC FACTS

◇ VENUS

Venus represents a similar situation in that its struggle for survival is clearly ongoing, but it is less of a personal matter in many ways, with the corporate society assuring stability for the long-term terraforming programs. The human intensity that is released does not disappear, however, but is instead sublimated into the formal and hierarchical Venusian lifestyle. Outsiders may find it vicious, but the average Venusian sees it as a worthy trade for the security offered by living under the umbrella of corporate paternalism. Venusians also are bound to their community by the need for localized arcology cities. If populations were not so confined, then the massive heat sinks that currently allow the planet to be inhabited would be impractical.

While the hostility of the Venusian environment is almost unparalleled, very little of that danger is borne by the individual. Indeed, with such a repressive environment, there is little need for publicly accessible airlocks and a correspondingly diminished chance of an accident. If it is not the job of a particular Venusian to maintain the systems that keep the arcology habitable, he is unlikely to give much thought to it on a day to day basis, an attitude strikingly different from that forced on many humans who have ventured away from the homeworld.

★ LIGHT OF DAY

Venus is distinctive for its orbit and spin that produces a single Venusian Day equivalent to 243 Earth days. The long periods of sunlight means there is little energy expended to light the arcologies. An arcology will have multiple atriums from the top to bottom of the structure. Each atrium is fitted with a mirror system to ensure light reaches every level of the atrium. Much of the arcology's agricultural production occurs under this directed sunlight in hanging gardens on each atrium level. Light is also directed into the interior spaces of the arcology by mirrors and fiber optic conduits. The surface of the arcology has numerous small sunlight collectors and deflectors that concentrate sunlight for interior lighting. Given the documented positive affects of natural light on human psychological well-being, many Venusians attribute the solar lighting to their ability to maintain a positive outlook on life.

◇ THE MOON

Earth's Moon sees two weeks of night followed by two weeks of day, causing extreme temperature variations. Also, the ever-present dust is still a problem for even the most hardened machinery. The gravity is weak enough that prolonged exposure, or simply being native-born, can jeopardize any hope of standing on humanity's mother planet. Only the satellite's proximity to Earth and the abundance of native resources made it a viable location for colonization. Selenites (as the Moon's inhabitants are known) had it especially hard during the Fall. While the goods they could produce and mine were well worth the exorbitant cost of keeping them alive on the Moon, the Fall robbed them of Earth's resources. No longer were vital organic products shuttled in regularly, and only the massive industrial base that had been used for mining purposes allowed the Selenites any chance of survival at all. While they did pull through, the tough times of the Fall have marked them cruelly, seemingly draining joy from life and converting it to a dry and determined pragmatism, regimented to preserve efficiency at all costs.

★ DOORS

Much of the present population lives in the habitats near the surface under the protection of radiation screens and micro-meteor point defense system. Despite their exposed position, the newer surface habitats are still engineered with due regard for safety. Large containment doors are conspicuous at the junction between every major section by the yellow and red warning strips that surrounds them. Every Selenite is careful to remain clear of the doors, and will politely ask anyone that does not to move to a safer location. When the emergency alarms sound, these fifteen centimeter thick doors begin to close rapidly within three seconds of the alarm's activation. Some non-Selenites could easily find themselves crushed in their panic to make it past a closing containment door.

MARS ◇

Mars is the most Earth-like of all the planets, and perhaps that explains why it has developed the most fractious political system; with abundance comes the luxury of internal conflict. While life in the Free Republic and the Federation differs greatly, there are some common threads. All Martians are more intensely connected than those on Venus to the terraforming projects that are slowly changing the world around them; the modifications on Mars are simply that much closer to a human scale. For instance, in the Republic, many homesteaders contribute to the process with their own terraforming plants and windcatchers. Martians are much more clearly masters of their own destiny. A visitor from Earth would find Mars the most welcoming among the other planets. Despite the need for cold weather gear and breathing apparatus, it is the only colonized planet to which they could relate.

Where the divide of politics crosses into daily life the change is dramatic. Few citizens of the Federation live outside the massive domed cities that provide shirtsleeve comfort for their inhabitants. It would be difficult for the Federation to maintain such tight control over its citizenry were they dispersed in the same manner as the fiercely individualistic Republicans. Republicans often have more material goods to their own name than their Federation counterparts, but it is correspondingly more likely that any given thing which they own is necessary and vital to their livelihood.

CITIES IN THE SAND ★

The domed cities of Mars are analogous to city states, though this definition applied to individual cities varies widely. The bylaws of any one city in the Free Republic will vary widely; while the bylaws of Federation cities are largely uniform between each and every city. These variances are especially evident in the migration and access policies applied to residents and visitors of the Martian domed cities. Some Free Republic cities allow unlimited freedom of movement to their residents, but visitors must undergo a lengthy process to apply a travel visa. Other Republic cities will unrestricted movement to anyone, resident or visitor. Federation citizens are issued resident identification for movement within a city, and are required to present it to law enforcement officers on demand. Some cities with critical industry and services must present their identification at checkpoints into designated areas. Individual buildings also require resident identification checks to gain entry. Federation citizens also require special travel identification when moving between domed cities with endorsements for access to public buildings.

OTHER BODIES ◇

Less substantive outcroppings of humanity can be found on some of the other major bodies in the Solar System. Titan is among the best known, but there are also people living on the Galilean satellites of Jupiter, the moons of Mars, and in several isolated science outposts on the satellites of the outer gas giants. Titan is the most startling of these bodies, so rich in hydrocarbons that it draws trade from throughout the Solar System to the isolated realm of Saturn. Almost 40,000 people call themselves Titanians, but only a much smaller number can hold claim to be ground-based "lifters," those who have truly braved the hydrocarbon muck and ethane lakes of the enshrouded moon. An even more elite group can claim to have seen Titan through only slightly less strenuous circumstances, by serving a scientific tour at *Alcott*, the IGS base on Titan.

Those living on the Galilean satellites of Jupiter have a far easier time than most. They live on the very doorstep of Olympus, an orbiting industrial base of unrivalled size and sophistication. Few choose to live permanently on the moons, instead serving short terms of service on these low-gee bodies. Most inhabitants are either scientists or workers on some industrial project, such as ice-mining on Europa. Other groundside stations support the Olympian leg of the Hanson Circuit or comprise elements of the civil and military deep-space communications network.

LIFELINES ★

A common element of both Titan and the Galilean satellites is the constant and regular arrival of ships bearing supplies and replacement personnel. Ships destined for Titan never make the trip empty in either direction. Though Titan is not completely self-reliant, the reliance of the inner planets on Titan's hydrocarbon resources ensures a regular schedule of ships arrive and depart from the Titanian Hydrocarbon Corporation stations orbiting Saturn's moon. Even with the assurance of regular visitations, Galilean and Titan facilities are striving to become as self-sufficient to lower the higher operational costs associated with shipping in needed supplies. THC has begun the construction of a Vivarium colony cylinder in orbit around Titan to meet this challenge.

HISTORICAL FACTS

SCIENTIFIC FACTS

LIVING IN SPACE

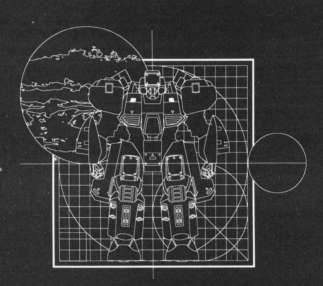

"It's not exactly like those old western movies, but living on
the frontier of this untamed land almost makes me want to
carry a six-shooter."

- Theo Meinz, Martian Terraformer

ARTIFICIAL ENVIRONMENTS ◄

It is not known how unique the Earth is throughout the galaxy, but its position amongst the planets and moons of the Solar System is unique and assured. No other environment can compare. No other body offers anything but unremitting hostility to human life. Nevertheless, in search of profit, adventure and freedom, humans have opened many of these worlds, and the void that lies between, to habitation. Some challenges remain to be conquered, beckoning further generations to press the borders of the possible further still, but the accomplishments of Humanity in the early twenty-third century are not to be taken lightly. Earth may still have the vast preponderance of Humanity's population, but Mars and Venus are both being terraformed, and hundreds of millions of people now live on colony cylinders, entire worldlets taken from the void.

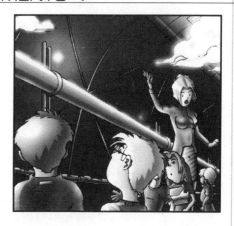

ENCLOSED SPACES ▼

When humans wanted to explore beyond the Moon's orbit, however, a solution was needed to provide sufficient atmosphere for the whole journey. That solution was to reduce the total pressure of the atmospheric gases people breathed from 1000 kilopascals to 34 kilopascals. The lower pressure atmosphere maintained the sea-level partial pressure of oxygen at 24 kilopascals with nitrogen occupying the remaining 10 kilopascals. This atmosphere has remained a standard for artificial environments since that time. Not only does it decrease the resources dedicated to sustaining the atmosphere, but it also solves numerous other problems: spacesuits can operate on this standard, thus eliminating the need to pre-breathe oxygen before EVAs, and structures can be more lightly-built since they do not need to contain higher atmospheric pressure.

Those that live in artificial environments would not normally experience seasonal changes in their environment; however, it was proven long ago that the lack of seasonal change has a detrimental affect on the human mind. To counteract this problem, the environment is often modified in small steps to simulate that changing conditions of an Earth-type seasonal round. Since there are numerous Earth-based variations to choose from, many artificial environments will cycle between two or three preferred choices, with each varied randomly by the environmental control systems. It is not uncommon for the population to vote for an extension of a particular seasonal cycle, or to change the choice of a seasonal cycle. Temperature, humidity, and hours of "daylight" are the most commonly modified environmental variables, but some environments do have the ability to provide some light precipitation. It is also common for a night not to be completely dark, but maintain a minimum level of lighting. Within colony cylinders, the effect of dawn and dusk is achieved by progressively modifying lighting levels from one end of the cylinder to the other.

COST OF LIVING ▼

The four major expenses are food, clothing, shelter and taxation. The latter is tied to the third by the maintenance, improvement and expansion of the artificial environments that people live within. Taxation is the first deduction from a person's monthly wages. Shelter is not really necessary within the controlled artificial environments many people live in; it is more an issue of having a personal private space. Food is no simple matter where the agricultural methods and species of Earth are ill-adapted to the restrictions of space. Though the human race is considered to have advanced greatly in the last few centuries, clothing is still a requirement.

AVERAGE TAXATION RATES ▥

Nation	Rate*	Nation	Rate*	Nation	Rate*
Mercury	10%	Venus	12%	Earth	35%
Orbitals	30%	Moon	25%	Mars Republic	5%
Mars Federation	50%	Jupiter	15%	Saturn	6%

* Percentage of annual income. Rates will vary by +/- 5 to 10% depending on income level and special cases.

2.1.1

2.1.2

2.1.2

▶ LIVING QUARTERS

Most locations in the Solar System have only a limited amount of space for living quarters. As a result, the design and arrangement of living quarters has become quite standardized, regardless of location. Nomad colonies and space stations are the least flexible in terms of the facilities available; living quarters are allocated based on position and number of occupants. These quarters are only of the most simple type (see *Basic Quarters* below). Normally, quarters do not have food preparation or personal hygiene facilities attached; it is much more space-efficient to have common food and hygiene facilities. Other locales offer a few more options (see *Expanded Quarters* below). It is entirely up to the owner's personal taste and means to decide how much space and additional amenities they want to pay for. Since living quarters are not usually designed to be modular, there are often waiting lists to get into a specific living arrangement.

Most living quarters are only available for a monthly rental rate. The only quarters available for permanent ownership are higher-end quarters such as certain expanded quarters or those built and owned by wealthy individuals. The rates vary not only with the size, but also by the location and the quality of the common facilities available at that location. Relatively speaking, renting quarters is very reasonably priced under the rent control laws enacted by most local governments. The cost of utilities (electricity, water, PAN access) is often included with the rental fee, except in Nomad colonies and other out-of-the-way places, where the value of electricity and water results in steep charges. All living quarters are grouped together to centralize access to resources.

▼ MINIMAL QUARTERS

Minimal quarters are the often only thing available to people with low wages, or those wishing to save some credits. A minimal living assignment is often part of the employment agreement for those that work some of the bottom-rung positions (such as unskilled labor). This actually saves the company money, since it can rent a large number of minimal living-space assignments at a significant discount compared to the cost of paying the workers additional wages for living-space rental. Minimal quarters are available in two flavors: "coffin rooms" and "square holes."

Coffin rooms: more properly know as sleeping tubes, are one-meter-diameter cylinders approximately two and a half meters long. This is little more than enough room for one person and a few belongings. The far end of the tube is small storage cabinet for a few personal effects like clothing and personal hygiene items. The mattress is a foam pad with a cloth cover and sheet for bedding. The bedding is changed after each occupant leaves; the occupant can also arrange for bedding changes every few days. The tube has a PAN adapter, but no access terminal is provided. There are also environmental controls for the tube: light, temperature and humidity.

Square Holes: more properly known as box quarters, have a double door entrance and are one and a half meters high and one and a half meters wide by three meters deep. These larger quarters are much more suitable for long-term habitation for those with a lower income. It is possible for two people to cohabitate in box quarters. Box quarters have features similar to sleeping tubes: foam mattress, bedding exchange, PAN adapter and environmental controls. There is, however, significantly more storage space at the back of the quarters for personal items.

Access to a sleeping tube or box quarters is granted when the user enters their identification or credit card. Sleeping tubes are rented on a monthly basis for 200 to 300 credits; nightly rates will vary from 8 to 12 credits. Because box quarters are considered low-cost, long-term quarters, they are rented on monthly basis for 300 to 400 credits.

◼ PLAYER CHARACTER LIFESTYLES

Player Characters need someplace to live when they are not out and about in the Solar System. Most PCs will have basic quarters, but this will not necessarily be the case for every PC. If the Player Character has the income to support more extensive lodgings, they can certainly live in something quite luxurious. Characters may also decide to maintain multiple residences for differing purposes. For those involved in covert operations and espionage, extra residences can act as safe houses or used as a base. For those with multiple identities, a residence is used to establish cover identities. For individuals that travel extensively, access to multiple residences means they always have someplace to stay.

COMMON FACILITIES ▥

Without a kitchen to prepare food, a bathroom for waste disposal, or showers for cleaning one's person, most people use the common facilities made available within the building their quarters are located in. Since most buildings have multiple floors of the same housing type, the floor layouts will be similar with bathroom and shower facilities located at different points on the floor. Essentially, each bathroom and shower unit is assigned to quarters closest to the facilities. Each unit has enough room to accommodate at least one-third of the assigned people at a single time. Access is granted by fingerprint scan to prevent problems such as surprise encounters, but anyone living on the floor can use any unit if it is not in use already. Mess halls or cafeterias are normally located on the lower floors of the building and can seat a majority of the building's residents at any one time. It is expected that those who arrive early will vacate their seat before the latecomers are ready to sit down.

BASIC QUARTERS ▼

Basic quarters are available for both single and double occupancy. Single basic quarters are rectangular rooms two meters wide by three meters long and two meters high. Double basic quarters are rectangular rooms three meters wide by four meters long and two meters high. These quarters are extremely functional and compact. Common to all living quarters, whatever the room size, is a storable bed that folds up against one of the room's walls. The bottom of the bed contains a fold-down desktop and storage areas for small personal effects. Standard to all quarters is a chair (or two), PAN access terminal, voice and video communications, video wall screen and a fairly significant amount of storage space for such a small area. People rarely use more storage space than what they receive with their quarters. Additional storage space is rented at a rate of 5 credits per month per cubic meter. The room has polymer panels that can be replaced — for a fee equal to 50% of one month's rent — to change the wall colors and textures. Environmental controls for light, temperature and humidity are standard. Monthly rent for single-occupancy quarters is 600 to 800 credits, while double-occupancy quarters rent for 900 to 1200 credits. If the quarters have a window to the exterior, the monthly rent is usually increased by about 200 credits.

HOTELS ▥

Hotels offer both minimal and basic quarters to travelers or others who require temporary lodging. By far, the most common hotel accommodations are the so-called "coffin hotels" that feature several corridors of sleeping tubes. Hotels offering box and basic quarters are much less common, since anyone requiring these kinds of facilities is likely to rent one on a longer term from a rental agent. If hotels do have either box or basic quarters available, the single-night rates range from approximately 20 credits for box quarters to 35-75 credits for basic quarters (single to double occupancy). In many cases, hotels offering these accommodations are simply normal quarters left vacant for rentals by daily use. All businesses offering daily rates will accept reservations for quarters. Although a few luxury hotels (like Joshua's Station's famed Parnassus Hotel) can be found here and there, they are very rare and very expensive (starting from several hundred credits per night).

BASIC ROOM FLOOR PLANS ▥

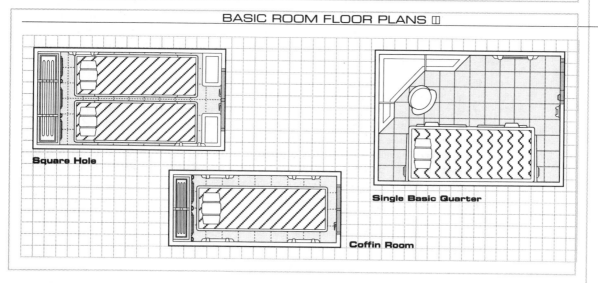

Square Hole

Single Basic Quarter

Coffin Room

▶ EXPANDED QUARTERS

Expanded quarters are, quite simply, basic single- or double-occupancy quarters with additional living areas attached. The interior of most buildings cannot be reconfigured, but there are some that are modular in design and can accommodate a modified floor plan. Other buildings are built with a variety of floor plans beyond the basic quarters. If the renter is not taking possession of an existing set of quarters, there is a reconfiguration fee equal to 10% of a single year's rent for the new floor plan. Not all of the expansion options in the table are available in every location; that is more a function of which options the building was designed to accept. All options have the same ceiling height as the rest of the quarters; two meters is standard.

⊞ EXPANSION OPTIONS

ADDITIONAL AREA	ADDS	SIZE	COST/MONTH
Bathroom I	toilet, sink	1 meter by 1 meter	200 credits
Bathroom II	toilet, sink, shower	1 meter by 2 meters	500 credits
Bathroom III	toilet, sink, bathtub w/shower	2 meters by 2 meters	1200 credits
Kitchen I	small-size fridge, two-element stove, cupboards	1 meter by 2 meters	350 credits
Kitchen II	average-size fridge, four element stove and oven, cupboards	2 meters by 2 meters	800 credits
Dining Area I	4-person seating	2 meters by 2 meters	450 credits
Dining Area II	8-person seating	3 meters by 3 meters	800 credits
"Living Room" I	two love seats, video wall screen	2 meters by 3 meters	600 credits
"Living Room" II	two couches, video wall screen	3 meters by 3 meters	900 credits
Extra Bedroom I	single bed	1.5 meters by 2 meters	400 credits
Extra Bedroom II	double bed	2 meters by 2 meters	500 credits
Entranceway	extra space at quarter's entrance	1 meter by 1.5 meters	300 credits
Storage Area	closet-type area	1 meter by 1 meter	200 credits
Private Study	desk w/terminal, chair, video wall screen, shelves	2 meters by 2 meters	750 credits

▶ WEALTHY QUARTERS

For those who have the money for something beyond the usual living quarters, there are no restrictions to what credits can buy. The quarters of the wealthy are always custom-built, but opportunities for construction are limited to new buildings and existing buildings being rebuilt or renovated. Since most of the wealthy who want to build quarters will have the money to either finance a new building or purchase an old one, it is not uncommon for this kind of thing to happen based on the individual's desire to set up new quarters. Some buildings are specifically designed with the goal of providing the space for a wealthy individual to design their quarters. Being very modular, the only real limitation to setting up the floor plan is an existing set of living quarters being in the way.

One of the greatest distinctions between wealthy quarters and other quarters is the finishing. Floors are covered in carpet, hardwood or tile. The walls have a textured finish or wood paneling. Rugs and tapestries are commonly added to rooms. Moldings and finishing are done in wood or stone. More open space gives the quarters an entirely different feel; very common to the quarters of the wealthy are numerous windows providing a view to the outside of the building. Combined with three-meter high ceilings, these types of quarters are cathedral-like in comparison to lesser living spaces.

Free-standing, dedicated-use furniture is another feature of wealthy quarters; there are no storable beds or folding tables. Couches, chairs, tables, desks, potted plants, beds and other such items of furniture are found throughout. Kitchens and bathrooms are two more amenities standard to these quarters. Though the wealthy would likely not cook themselves, many will have a chef do the cooking for them. The other option for those quarters lacking a kitchen is to have catered meals delivered. Given this, a dining room is a standard feature for enjoying one's meal; the dining room will usually seat anywhere from eight to twenty-four people, sometimes more. The last common feature is at least one full bath; on a space station where water rationing is always strict, a bath is often seen as the most excessive symbol of wealth.

Given the widely varying nature of these quarters, and the fact that most are purpose built, they are not available for rent, except on an individual basis. The purchase price for these kinds of quarters can range from 500,000 to 3,000,000 credits. Because they are not a rental property, wealthy quarters are subject to an annual property tax by the local government. The tax rate can vary widely from 10% to 30% of the evaluated price of the property.

FOOD AND DRINK ▼

For most of the population in the Solar System, meals are taken in a common area. This practice saves resources in a number of areas — space, energy and waste. The meals available are highly nutritious and well balanced, so that even those performing a minimum level of daily activity will remain relatively healthy. The reason for such nutritious food is the nature of that food: everything is made with specially produced and processed ingredients to optimize the health benefits. Typical meals are pre-prepared and packaged with a variety of choices. Most of the meal's protein comes from high-density aquaculture and soy, and other ingredients are provided from high-yield, high-density crops of grains and rice. Specialty crops of fruits and vegetables are grown with hydroponics or private gardens (see below). All of these are combined to provide quick, nutritional food for the most people with the minimum required resources.

Cafeterias and mess halls are normally located on the ground floor of a living quarters complex, and serve only processed foods. Since there are normally people working or doing business at all hours, the facility does not have the room to seat everyone, and those that arrive early are expected to finish their meals by the time the late arrivals need a place to sit down. Business complexes have a cafeteria to serve lunches and other meals. People have the choice to purchase meals either as singles or part of a meal plan. Meal plans provide a limited choice of menu, but offer a 10% discount over purchasing single meals. Naturally produced and prepared foods are only available in restaurants, and are considered a treat by most. A typical restaurant meal will cost double the pre-packaged equivalent, but there is a wider variety of specialty foods like beef, large crustaceans and fish. Vegetables and fruits are prepared in a traditional manner that is firmly geared toward creating something that tastes different from the normal packaged equivalents. The skill of the preparation varies widely, however, and many say that good chefs are most abundant on Venus and Mars.

Microgravity makes eating an entirely different experience. Food that gets loose in microgravity makes a large mess that can escape in any direction. Those people with plenty of microgravity experience can get away with eating from open containers, but the traditional squeeze bulbs and dry foods of the early Space Age are still available for the rest. Since most ships have some way of producing at least minimal gravity for the long voyages they undertake, microgravity foods are normally reserved for when acceleration is not available, or when there is an emergency situation. While everyone seems to enjoy complaining about the quality of these foods, no one seems to complain too loudly when they are truly hungry.

UNIQUE TASTES ★

One would not think of Mars as the premier producer of fine wine in the Solar System. However, genetic manipulation has adapted Earth grapevines to Martian conditions. The independent wineries of Mars reproduce many of the great vintages of past, in addition to new wines unique to Mars — like the Martian Red, Green and Blue. These can have virtually any combination of qualities and flavors. The former wine-producing areas of the Kingdom of France are either engaged in sustenance agriculture or environmental recovery projects. The small quantity of French wine is reserved for consumption by the nobility.

Most people who live in an artificial environment would agree that garden-grown vegetables are the best-tasting of foods. The roofs of many colony cylinder buildings are flat and are covered in soil or hydroponics gardens. Except for the smallest buildings, employees or residents usually spend time tending these gardens for a portion of the harvest. Underground settlements on the Moon and Mercury use potted plants — again, fruits and vegetables — to brighten the surroundings. If the plant is located in a public area, it is considered extremely rude to take a sample unless first offered a taste by the owner or caretaker.

FOOD AND DRINK ▯

PROCESSED FOODS	COST	FRESH FOODS	COST	UNIQUE TASTES	COST
Soy burger	3 cr	Fresh fruit	10 cr	Mars Classic Earth Wines	50-300 cr
Bottled water (1L)	1 cr	Fruit drink (1L)	5-10 cr	Mars Red Wine	20-60 cr
Packaged breakfast	4-6 cr	Dairy milk (1L)	15 cr	Mars Green Wine	40-120 cr
Packaged lunch	7-10 cr	Seafood meal	25-120 cr	Mars Blue Wine	75-200 cr
Package dinner	9-12 cr	Steak meal	30-150 cr		
Energy bar	1 cr				
Soy milk	2 cr				

Note: fresh foods are often less expensive on planets and farming-oriented colonies, and more expensive in isolated areas.

LIVING IN SPACE

▶ CLOTHING

For most people living in space, clothing choice is often a tradeoff between aesthetics and functionality. In some cases functionality is paramount, while for others it is the opposite. In the end, the most common feature is the synthetic fabrics used to manufacture clothing. Only Earth has the space and resources for the production of natural fibers, and most of this clothing remains on Earth; in fact, most spacers think that producing natural fiber clothing is an unnecessary waste of resources.

People avoid wearing loose or baggy clothes almost entirely; clothes with drape have a tendency to catch on things and cause accidents, especially in low gravity and confined spaces. This aversion to flamboyance also grew out of the need to conserve resources. Even people who live and work in relatively spacious environments wear fitted clothes. It is only on singular occasions of great celebration, such as marriage, that this unwritten rule of fashion is ignored, and then not always.

Work clothing fits into one of two categories: office and everything else. Functionality and durability are the two qualities most people seek in their work clothes. For people in technical occupations, the work coverall is most common work outfit; the spacesuit is second. Work coveralls have a multitude of pockets, both large and small, and numerous loops and straps for attaching tools and more pockets. Top-quality coveralls use fire retardant cloth that effectively reduces a fire's Intensity by two. Office clothing is designed to be sharp, clean looking and comfortable.

Casual clothing is meant to be comfortable above all else. After spending the day in the tight confines of a spacesuit, people like something relaxing to wear. Stylish coveralls and one-piece body suits made with supple fabrics are the most common casual clothing. Slacks and shirts of all cuts are also common. Zero-gravity clothing is usually body-hugging, but loose clothing will have elasticized cuffs to keep sleeves and pants legs in place.

Where there is gravity, there are still tuxedos and gowns to be worn. Most people don't have the storage space for formal clothing, so rentals are common. One popular fashion trend has incorporated micro-actuators with a small processor and power source to create "living" clothing. The variations in style and motion encompass everything from the curious to the provocative. Also popular are video or holographic membranes, that can be used to display virtually any image within the limits of social convention and legality.

☐ CLOTHING

ITEM	COST	ITEM	COST
Work Coverall	75 cr	Casual Pants	30-80 cr
Fire-Retardant Coverall	125 cr	Casual Shirt	20-50 cr
Business Suit	200-400 cr	Evening Gown	200-800 cr
Casual Business Clothes	100-200 cr	Tuxedo	400 cr, rental 30 cr/day
Casual Coverall	50-100 cr	Fashionable Clothing	500-2500 cr

◀ Fashionable Jovian Business Attire

◀ CEGA Business Suit

◀ Spacer Work

▶ Casual Business Suit

▶ Fashionable Clothing

▶ Spacesuit

UNIFORMS ▼

Uniforms are not just for the military and paramilitary services, though these uniforms are the most recognizable as such. The principal purpose of a uniform is identification of the person's affiliation to an organization. Whether the uniform has any functionality related to the performance of a person's duties is dependent upon said duties. Military uniforms are divided into two classes: duty and dress. Duty uniforms are day-to-day personal wear and are oriented toward functionality. For example, a technician's duty uniform has large pockets and is reinforced at the knees, shoulders and elbows. Dress uniforms are reserved for more formal occasions such as inspections or military receptions. They are much more formal, displaying rank, decorations, and unit affiliations. (See **Jovian Chronicles Companion**, pages 47 to 53 for insignias and decorations.)

MILITARY UNIFORM COLORS

NATION	DUTY UNIFORM	DRESS UNIFORM
Jovian	White and gray with yellow piping	White long jacket with gold piping
CEGA	Light olive	Black long coat with silver piping
Venusian	Charcoal	Gray and gold ceremonial armor, cape with corporate colors
Mercurian	Light blue	Dark blue jacket and pants with red piping
Mars Federation	Rust red with black mottle	Crimson jacket with gold piping, black pants
Mars Free Republic	Rust red with dark gray mottle with green spots	Dark green desert cloak with gold clasps and buckles

COMMUNICATIONS ◄

With the huge volumes of information being transferred on a daily basis, the infrastructure to support that transfer requires constant maintenance, improvement and expansion. As such, there are user fees associated with using voice and video communications as well as for accessing the SysInstruum through a public access network (PAN). There are two types of communication connections a user can establish: internal and external. Internal connections are made between two access points within a single station, colony cylinder or settlement. External connections are made between two access points in two different stations, cylinders or settlements within a local area of space or planetary surface. For security reasons, any direct access to external SysInstruum nodes is forbidden. (i.e. no external access via PAN connection.) A user can make a special request for access to specific information and searches.

INTERPLANETARY COMMUNICATIONS ▼

Interplanetary communication is not an instantaneous occurrence between the planets. Even the closest planets require almost an hour for a message to make the trip there and back. The different orbital periods and distances require that multiple communication arrays are aligned with different points in space, including relay satellites when line-of-sight is blocked. The cost is calculated using the square root of the distance expressed as millions of kilometers. For example, a message transmitted 160 million kilometers will cost 12.6 credits per minute (square root of 160 = 12.6). A table of closest, average and farthest orbital distances between the planets can be found on pages 168 and 169 of the **Jovian Chronicles** rulebook.

COMMUNICATION ACCESS FEES

LOCATION/METHOD	INTERNAL ACCESS FEE	EXTERNAL ACCESS FEE
Personal Quarters		
Voice	Free	0.1 credit/minute
Video	0.1 credit/minute	0.2 credit/minute
PAN Access	0.1 credit/minute	5 credits/minute*
Public Comm Terminal		
Voice	0.2 credit/minute	0.3 credit/minute
Video	0.3 credit/minute	0.7 credit/minute
PAN Access	0.5 credit/minute	10 credits/minute*
Remote Access		
C-Link	0.1 credit/minute	n/a
PAN Access	1 credit/minute	15 credits/minute*

* Additional fees for special requests and information transmission

▶ GETTING AROUND

The cities of pre-Fall Earth were often choked with ground vehicles operating on millions of kilometers of roadways. The pollution, noise, maintenance costs and resources this system required make duplicating this kind of transportation system impossible elsewhere. As a result, highly efficient public transportation systems were necessary to handle the large populations of colony cylinders and other large facilities. Operations research specialists are continually working on improving the efficiency of public transportation systems. This has coincided with improved efficiency through advanced technology in developing transportation infrastructure. There are numerous payment options for the use of public transportation, with the cost varying little between locations. A six hour, unlimited-use pass costs one credit. Monthly passes are 40 credits, and annual passes are 400 credits.

Monorails form the basis of any colony cylinder's transportation infrastructure — extensive road systems require too much space and are too inefficient. The system places the monorail between quadrant boundaries with terminals located at the intersection of quadrants and the mid-point between intersections. Vivarium cylinders also have a monorail "subway" line that runs the length of the sunline for access to zero-gravity facilities and cargo transfer areas. Monorail cars are computer-controlled from an onboard system that coordinates monorail operations with a central computer. The system is has several redundancies that allow direct network operation through inter-car communications when the central computer is down; on the other hand, the central computer can take remote control of a car if the onboard system malfunctions.

Transit buses that run on fuel cells or superconducting batteries operate within the quadrants between the monorail lines of the colony cylinder. They usually run in circular routes that move people to and from the monorail stations. Varying in capacity from twenty to forty passengers, the buses allow quick access to areas that don't have immediate access to the monorail stations. The bus service also provides mobility to the elderly and disabled within the quadrant where they live. Within the largest space stations, or even smaller stations and surface habitats, small open cars that offer standing room only for ten to twenty passengers operate within the limited space available while still providing quick and efficient travel.

The Moon and Mars are the only two locations in the Solar System, other than Earth, that have **permanent surface transportation systems**; the nature of Venus' surface requires that all public transportation be airborne. Both have monorail systems that provide regularly scheduled service between major settlements. Numerous private companies provide schedules and charter travel services between smaller regional settlements using wheeled or tracked vehicles. On the Moon, modified OTVs called hoppers launch themselves into low-altitude ballistic trajectories between destinations.

▼ INTER-CYLINDER SHUTTLE

Regularly scheduled shuttle flights move people and goods between the clusters of colony cylinders throughout the Solar System. There are few people who commute between cylinders and stations for work, so it is sufficient to limit cargo capacity on some flights to accommodate extra passengers. If a shuttle is not carrying passengers, it is carrying cargo. Within a cluster, the round-trip fee is 15 credits per person or 100 kg of cargo, 10 if one-way. For service between clusters, the fee goes up to 35 credits (25 for one-way trips).

Shuttle passengers who reserve a seat at least twelve hours in advance are guaranteed a spot and receive a 15% discount. Passenger reservations after this deadline up to the departure time must pay the full fare and risk losing their seat to cargo shipments; after the deadline, cargo is given equal priority for passage.

▼ PERSONAL TRANSPORTATION

Ownership of a personal vehicle — beyond a bicycle or scooter — is very rare throughout the artificial environments people occupy in the Solar System; within space stations, the only personal transportation systems available are one's own legs. This does not mean there are not vehicles, but the majority of them are service and cargo vehicles. Colony commuters are compact reverse-tricycle or four-wheel vehicles that carry two to four people. The cost of owning, operating and parking these vehicles is very high compared to public transportation. Bicycles are a popular and inexpensive transportation choice. Designated bike lanes allow for quick travel with fewer worries about pedestrians and other hazards. Some colony cylinder administrations greatly favor bicycle riders by also provide public bicycle stations where a person can use their public transit pass to check out a bicycle. The person can then return the bicycle to any bicycle station, whether it be the same one or a station halfway across the cylinder.

EMERGENCIES ◀

When in space, one's life is constantly dependent on the condition of a mere few centimeters' thickness of hull plates, bulkheads and other synthetic materials. While there will always be accidents, spacers are particularly serious about taking the necessary precautions to limit the loss of life due to hazards such as decompression and fire. Whether these events occur as the result of combat, natural or intentional causes, decompression and fire have the greatest potential for causing casualties and fatalities within the artificial environments that humans call home in the Solar System.

Children learn and practice emergency procedures from the day they are old enough to understand the lessons. They learn to trigger alarms, summon help and seek shelter in cases of fire or severe drops in pressure. As they grow older, they learn basic firefighting and hull-repair techniques, and are also drilled to care for children younger than themselves. Ironically, children are the ones who often keep the adults well reminded of the need to practice safety, since the constant lessons make them happy to point out when adults are doing something incorrectly or in an unsafe manner. Smaller emergency spacesuits for children are located toward the floor in most lockers, should a child find need of a suit when an adult is not present.

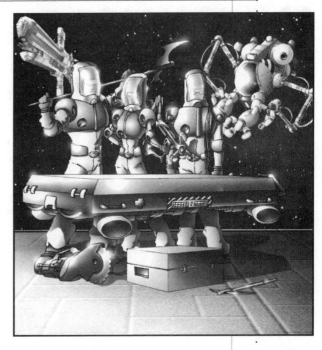

DECOMPRESSION ▼

While experiencing a decompression emergency can be terrifying, it is actually one of the most survivable of spaceborne mishaps. Contrary to popular belief, the human body can actually survive unprotected exposure in space for longer than a minute, though the victim will suffer increasingly severe physiological damage. Because preventing and containing rapid decompression is important for preserving valuable atmosphere and structural integrity, a great amount of energy and resources are devoted to developing methods for dealing with this type of emergency. Aboard military vessels during combat, all military personnel wear full spacesuits, and the vessel's atmosphere is lowered to near-vacuum conditions. This reduces damage and the loss of volatiles due to battle damage.

If a compartment undergoes decompression, remaining in the structure is the primary concern. Doing so allows rescue and damage control personnel to quickly find and assist personnel at the site of the incident (since a lengthy search decreases the odds of survival almost exponentially). In the case of rapid decompression — also know as a "blow out" — it is unlikely that personnel can make it through exit hatches before the hatches close to seal the area anyway, so staying in the structure provides the best chance for survival. Slow decompression, either due to a minute puncture or a faulty seal, is less dramatic (though still very serious) and allow for a greater number of options. The first is to exit the area before hatches and blast doors close to seal the area. An automated voice informs occupants of the time available to exercise this option. If there is insufficient time to exit the area, personnel must use an emergency spacesuit or survival bubble before they lose consciousness. The second option is to attempt to plug the leak or at least slow it down enough for help to arrive. The third option, a rather unpleasant and terrifying maneuver, is to hyperventilate to charge the bloodstream with oxygen and then attempt a "naked" spacewalk to another pressurized area such as an airlock (obviously, this option is not always available, and require serious nerve to commit to).

After personnel have seen to their own safety, and assisted others, the next action is to contact the designated emergency response authority to advise them of the situation. Personnel trained in damage control procedures can assess the situation for possible temporary repairs and begin the necessary work if the correct equipment for doing so is available. All personnel are to remain in the decompressed area until they are escorted from the area by rescue or damage control personnel; alternatively, personnel must follow evacuation procedures if contact with personnel outside the decompressed cannot be established. Under no circumstances are personnel to open sealed hatches and blast doors, as this could compromise the integrity of the entire vessel and the safety of other spacers.

2.7.1

☆ DECOMPRESSION AND THE HUMAN BODY

At the beginning of Humankind's ascent into space during the 20th century, experiments were conducted to determine the effects of exposure to vacuum. The results showed that exposure to space for about thirty seconds is unlikely to cause permanent injury. However, holding one's breath is likely to damage one's lungs; full exhalation is recommended. Direct exposure of the skin to the intense ultraviolet radiation of the sun will cause severe sunburn. Lengthy exposure is likely to cause decompression sickness. Symptoms include mild, reversible and painless swelling of the skin and the tissue beneath. After prolonged vacuum exposure, the blood's supply of oxygen is depleted, so lack of oxygen will render the victim unconscious after a minute or two, with brain damage and death following very quickly. The body will not explode, nor does the blood boil because of the structural and environmental protection of the skin and circulatory system. One will not instantly freeze, because although space is cold, there is no medium for heat to transfer away from the body. However, the saliva on the tongue and other external body fluids will boil because of the extremely low vapor pressure at body temperature.

▼ FIRE

Fire is the one of the most feared emergencies in an artificial environment. It is not the heat of the flames that poses the greatest danger, but rather the fire's voracious appetite for oxygen and the smoke, carbon dioxide and other compounds that quickly fill the air. A fire aboard a vessel can quickly consume valuable oxygen and pollute the entire vessel's atmosphere, making even a small fire hazardous. The relatively high concentration of oxygen compared to nitrogen in the standard artificial atmosphere means that fires burn with greater intensity and spread more rapidly than under normal earthbound conditions. All buildings and spacecraft are built to contain fires; rooms are layered with fire retardant materials, and all doors are equipped to close automatically when a fire alarm is tripped. Occupants can open a door to exit the room if the sensors on the opposite side deem it safe to do so (based on temperature and air quality).

The preferred option for controlling and extinguishing fires is to evacuate the atmosphere in the immediate area after it is sealed off. Both ships and buildings within open environments (like colony cylinders and surface settlements), are compartmentalized to facilitate the containment of a fire. The atmosphere is then evacuated completely, or the section is flooded with an inert gas to "starve" the flames. Emergency oxygen apparatus for use by trapped personnel is stored in lockers at containment doorways and other strategic locations. Emergency spacesuits can also be used to limit exposure to fire by-products. As a primary or backup system, wet or dry chemical fire-suppression systems are installed in critical areas; some materials can be self-oxidizing, or may be in contact with an oxidizer, so that evacuating the atmosphere will not extinguish some fires without a fire suppression system. (See the **Space Equipment Handbook**, page 43, for more information about fire fighting equipment.)

Within large, open environments like colony cylinders and surface domes, fires that occur or spread outside a building are combated by variety of methods. Buildings are equipped with exterior chemical fire-suppression systems to prevent the spread of a fire from building to building. Colony cylinder sunlines are equipped with fire retardant foam bombs that can be dropped and directed onto open fires. If there is a sufficiently large population present, emergency response teams equipped for fire fighting duties are available. The environmental systems of buildings are also capable of reverse operations to extract impurities from the surrounding air. Mobile air quality conditioners can be brought into place to prevent the contamination of the habitat's atmosphere.

Some settlements and cylinders also have emergency response M-bots that will automatically respond to alarms with a minimum of human intervention. Most of these are modified search and rescue drones that, although too expensive to qualify as 'disposable', are tough and smart enough to do the job safely. They are equipped with laser cutters and powerful fire extinguisher systems, along with extensive protection against environment hazards. The M-Bots generally have four or more legs for improved stability, with small thrusters providing mobility in space. A number of drones acting autonomously can follow a search pattern and alert an operators if they find anything, at which point they can be tele-operated for finer control. Some can be controlled in the field by a properly-equipped exo-suit. See **Mechanical Catalog 2** for stats and background on these.

EVACUATION ▼

The evacuation of several million people from a colony cylinder is the worst nightmare of disaster services across the Solar System. There is little chance of evacuating an entire colony cylinder, or surface habitat, without some fatalities; in fact, emergency planners know that there will likely be many deaths, and do not publicize that fact. No cylinder has the lifeboats, spacesuits, or survival bubbles to evacuate the entire population. The reality is that if a cylinder is so damaged as to require total and immediate evacuation, it is likely that a great majority of the population will be dead or dying before they have a chance to evacuate. In an emergency, the evacuation alarms will sound and provide instructions for moving to lifeboats and airlocks. Emergency services run evacuation drills in a random cylinder quadrant every few months to ensure citizens are familiar with the evacuation procedures. The situation on Venus, the Moon and Mars is very different, comparatively. (Refer to *Evacuation*, page 41 and 42 in the **Space Equipment Handbook**, for more information.)

VENUS ◇

On Venus, evacuation to the surface is not a viable option for a large portion of the population. Mobile emergency shelters that are lowered to the surface are only accessible to people on the lowest levels. Self-contained emergency shelters are located at regular intervals within the habitat's interior areas. The upper surfaces of the settlements are equipped with a variant of the surface mobile shelter. These shelters use rockets and deployable wings to lift the shelter away from the habitat on a course for a neighboring habitat. The shelters are capable of landing on the surface, where they have an operational lifespan for twenty-four hours.

THE MOON ◇

On the Moon, heavily compartmentalized constructions, with survival shelters both inside and outside, serve to protect the inhabitants. There are sufficient self-contained emergency shelter spaces to protect at least 75% of the expected population of the section for the full support lifespan of the shelter. Exterior airlocks have a large supply of emergency spacesuits nearby to allow the rapid evacuation of large numbers of people. (See below for more on airlock use during evacuations.) Emergency shelters are also located along commonly traveled routes between settlements. It is considered a criminal offense to use the shelters in non-emergency situations.

MARS ◇

On Mars, immediate evacuation is easier to conduct under the partially terraformed conditions, which allow people to simply leave with clothing and oxygen masks. This simplicity gives evacuees the chance to set up deployable emergency shelters, or be picked up and moved to another habitat nearby. Larger settlements that have several interconnected habitats will evacuate to adjacent habitats. The primary concern of rescue workers is to minimize long-term exposure to the Martian environment. As on the moon, emergency shelters are also located along commonly traveled routes between settlements.

SPACE ◇

Besides the use of lifeboats and shelters to protect the lives of a habitat's citizens, airlocks are used as egress points from dangerous situations within the habitat. Procedure for evacuation from an airlock begins with getting as many people as possible into emergency or regular spacesuits or survival bubbles in the corridor outside the airlock, and then to seal the corridor. The airlock atmosphere is evacuated, and one section of the interior door is opened, lowering the corridor pressure. The exterior door is opened by overriding the controls. Once the atmosphere in the corridor has finished venting, people exit the habitat with people in spacesuits carrying out the people in survival bubbles. (See *Airlocks* on page 51 for more information about operating airlocks.)

TRAVELING IN SPACE

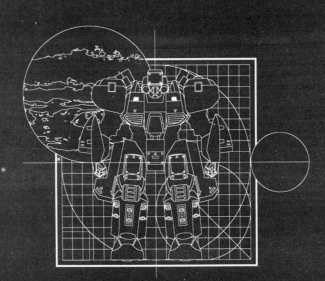

Identification, ticket and passport please.
Please place your luggage on the table.
— Universal greeting of customs and
immigration officers everywhere

CIVILIAN SPACE TRAVEL ◀

While the militaries send their fleets about the Solar System, many times that number of civilian vessels are travelling about the Solar System at any given moment. The majority of these ships are carrying cargo, but there are many vessels that also carry passengers. Most passenger craft carry a mixture of cargo and passengers, since there are relatively few vessels built exclusively for passenger travel.

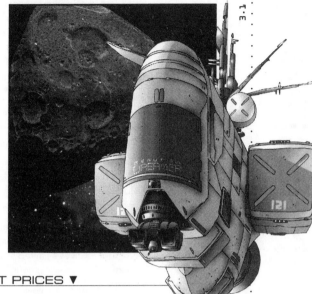

Fares for passenger and cargo travel are based on mass and distance traveled, and also by the type or class of travel. Customs and immigration inspections are always required to ensure that the rules of travel and commerce are followed. For people travelling between the planets, there are pre- and post-journey activities, as well the journey itself. Even with the rhetoric flying between CEGA and Jovian politicians, the amount of traffic within the Solar System has never been higher. At the same time, the increasing amounts of cheap arms on the market — legally and illegally — have made some routes more susceptible to pirate attacks.

TICKET PRICES ▼

The base fare for interplanetary passenger travel is equal to the square root of the distance traveled in kilometers. For example, a journey between Earth and Mars is 272.6 million kilometers on average (see the **Jovian Chronicles Rulebook**, page 168). Therefore, the base fare is the square root of 272.6 million, which equals 16,510 credits. This base fare is then subject to a Transit Multiplier based on the Class the passengers will be traveling. First Class passage costs 4 times the base fare; Second Class passage costs 2.5 times the base fare; Business Class passage costs 2.5 times the base fare; Third Class passage costs 2 times the base fare; Economy Class passage costs 1.5 times the base fare; finally, Sleeper Class passage costs 0.5 times the base fare. For passengers with Build greater than +2, an additional multiplier of 1.5 is applied for each point Build above +2; for those with a Build of less than -2, an additional multiplier of 0.75 is applied for each point of Build below -2.

Cargo over the limit allowed by the paid passage is allowed, and carries a rate increase of 25% of the fare per 20% increment of additional cargo. For example, the charge for transporting 200% of the allowed cargo limit is equal to 125% of the passenger's fare. The actual fare can also vary from as little as 50% to more than 200% depending on factors like planetary positions and re-mass burn rates. Shortened transit times will always cost more due to fuel costs. Though there are few circumstances that would cause a passenger line to schedule a faster-than-normal trip, it does occur occasionally, with a proportional increase in the base fare.

LIFTING AND DESCENT FEES ◇

For those who require transportation between a planetary surface and orbit, there are lifting and descent fees for passage to and from orbit. There is a single price for lifting from, and returning to, surface locations. Purchasing both lift and descent tickets simultaneously provides a discount of 25% over the purchase of two individual fares. For those traveling to and from orbit via the Venus and Earth skyhooks, tickets are discounted by 25% for the fuel savings granted by the skyhook. The modifiers for Build given above are also applied to lifting and descent fees. Cargo fees for passenger baggage are equal to a single ticket as a percentage of 75 kilograms. For example, a passenger lifting 50 kilograms from Earth will pay 66% of the usual 845 credit fee, or 558 credits (rounded up).

LIFTING AND DESCENT FEES TABLE ▯

Location	Lifting Fee	Descent Fee	Location	Lifting Fee	Descent Fee
Mercury	313 cr	157 cr	Venus	772 cr	1220 cr
Earth	845 cr	845 cr	Moon	178 cr	89 cr
Mars	386 cr	231 cr	Titan	198 cr	242 cr

TRAVELING IN SPACE

▼ PASSENGER ACCOMMODATIONS

First Class fare entitles the passenger to a private suite (two or three rooms) located in the gravity wheel, if the vessel is equipped with one. The suite will likely have several windows providing an exterior view of the ship. Having paid the most for their passage, First Class passengers receive priority access to all shipboard amenities such as theaters, restaurants, game rooms, lounges and personal services. All of these services (with the possible exception of meals) are included with the fare. First Class passengers also receive room service. Each First Class passenger is allowed 300 kilograms of cargo.

Second Class fare entitles the passenger to a cabin with a private bathroom likely located in the gravity wheel, but without an exterior window. Access to common facilities is provided at a greatly discounted user fee. Second Class passengers receive a good selection of meal plans. Each Second Class passenger is allowed 200 kilograms of cargo.

Business Class fare offers business travelers less cargo allowance, but provides high-priority access to onboard computer and communication facilities. They receive the same cabin assignments and meal plan choices as Second Class travelers, but the common facilities available are more geared toward the working business person, with the fees adjusted accordingly. Each Business Class passenger is allowed 50 kilograms of cargo.

Third Class offers the passenger limited privacy in a small private cabin with compact shower and sanitary facilities. The cabin is little more than a storage locker for the passenger's cargo and a sleeping bag. The passenger receives a limited selection of meal options, and does not receive a discount on the user fees for recreation and entertainment facilities. Each Third Class passenger is allowed 50 kilograms of cargo.

Economy Class fares provide the passenger with basic meals and dormitory-style sleeping arrangements that vary from two to eight people per room. Economy Class passengers are restricted from some facilities, and do not receive any discounts. Each Economy Class passenger is limited to 20 kilograms of cargo.

Cryogenic Storage, or Sleeper Class, is available as the most inexpensive form of passenger travel. The passenger spends most of the voyage in a semi-comatose state monitored by the ship's computer and medical personnel; they are woken regularly for exercise and medical checkups, but do not receive meals or entertainment. Sleeper accommodations are available in both the hull and gravity wheel, to maintain the health of travelers from different locales. Each Sleeper Class passenger is allowed 50 kilograms of cargo.

▥ PASSENGER SERVICES

There are many companies offering passenger services between the planets at any one time. Numerous independent vessels offer service on irregular schedules that are posted on the SysInstruum. People who don't mind taking a little longer to travel to their destination can sometimes find a berth on a Mercurian Merchant Guild sail ship, though normal practice requires passengers to work with the crew as part of the passage price.

The Venusian company Eclipse Travel is the largest company to offer regularly scheduled service between the inner planets. The Jovian company Galileo Spacelines offers travelers scheduled service between the Jovian states and the inner Solar System in addition to bimonthly service between the Jovian states. Smaller companies such as Trans-Planet (Earth), Inner System (Venus) and Universal (Mars) offer travelers a choice in service between the company's home planet and one or two other planets.

White Star Line is a name associated with the greatest transportation disaster of the 20th century, the sinking of the RMS *Titanic*. While the company has no plans to attach the name to any of its vessels, White Star Line is concentrating its business on "glamour" cruises between the inner and outer Solar System. Using a series of gravity-assist maneuvers around the inner planets and Sun, the vessels take scenic tours through the inner Solar System before traveling to Saturn for another gravity assist that returns the vessel to Jupiter. The trip back to the inner system is via a direct route. The accommodations offered are limited to First, Second, Third, and Sleeper Class passage at double the normal Transit Multiplier.

The Hanson Circuit is the main passenger service between the Jovian states. Attaching themselves to the two-kilometer-long booster sleds, short-range vessels called sled-liners move people and materials across the vast distance separating the three states of the Confederation. Most passengers travel Sleeper class for an inexpensive average price of 1000 credits for a one-way ticket between states. For those that make the trip awake, the ticket will cost between 44,000 credits (Economy Class) and 120,000 credits (First Class). (Refer to the **Jupiter Planet Sourcebook**, page 49, for more information on the Hanson Circuit.) Other passenger services between the states are irregularly scheduled and take significantly longer to arrive.

THE JOURNEY ◄

Passengers require three things before they can board the vessel. First is their personal identification and any related travel documents for entering and leaving the nation that they depart from or arrive at. Second is their ticket. Finally they require a medical certificate that states their ability, or inability, to live in low- or zero-gee conditions, and any health concerns that the medical staff should be aware of. Sleeper Class passengers must undergo an additional medical exam to determine if they are fit to endure long-term somnolence without severe adverse affects (Sleeper passengers are always warned that Sleeper travel is physically taxing and may produce harmful side-effects). Passengers who have problems with low gravity are treated with free drugs to allow them to embark and disembark from the vessel while it is docked.

Once the passenger has checked in at the spaceport entrance, they are directed to a room where they are instructed on basic safety and emergency procedures, and familiarized with the layout of the vessel. There is a brief exam at the conclusion of this one-hour presentation, with those who fail required to take an additional half-hour course and exam before being allowed to board. The authorities will not allow any passenger aboard the vessel who may endanger themselves, other passengers, the vessel, or the crew. Resistance from the passengers (rare among spacers) often results in their immediate blacklisting with the passenger line; they will not be allowed to purchase passage with that company in the future.

Following the safety and orientation session, passengers are directed to the customs and immigration inspection area. Customs officers ensure that the people leaving are allowed to do so, that they are not carrying anything that is illegal to transport, and check on any number of other regulations and rules that must be followed by travelers. Customs officers are permitted to perform random searches of any cargo a passenger is taking aboard the vessel. (See *Customs and Immigration* on the following page.)

Once passengers are cleared through customs and immigration, they are assisted to their quarters by ship stewards and courtesy personnel. Those passengers traveling Business Class or better can experience the departure from the various lounges in the passenger areas. During maneuvers they can be seated and secured in the numerous comfortable seating areas. All other passengers are required to remain in their cabins until departure maneuvers are completed. During maneuvers these passengers must secure themselves on their beds with safety netting. Once the departure maneuvers are complete, the ship's centrifuge (or the ship itself, depending on the vessel's design) is spun up to produce gravity in the passenger and crew areas.

DURING THE VOYAGE ◄

Once the final maneuvers and thrusting are complete, and gravity has been established, passengers are free to move about the designated passenger areas. This is also the first chance people get to eat after the trip starts as it is recommended to all that they skip eating until after departure. This reduces the chance of people throwing up their last meal during the zero-gravity conditions of boarding through to departure.

Stewards work hard throughout the voyage to keep the passengers fed and entertained. When passengers book their passage, part of the process is to complete a questionnaire about their favorite activities and other personal requirements when traveling. The questionnaire has all manner of questions about food, entertainment, hobbies and work activities, along with ample opportunity to make special requests. This information is compiled and used by the stewards to organize activities for the duration of the journey. Special requests may be provided for, but always for a fee proportional to the request.

For those that wish (or are required) to spend time in low- or zero-gravity, there are facilities for numerous activities from sports to simply floating and bouncing about. For those not acquainted with living in low gravity, these facilities are always heavily used if a person is traveling to a destination in constant low gravity. There are typically some passengers coming from low-gravity environments, so there are some quarters for these passengers so that they can acclimatize themselves to higher-gravity environments.

Passengers traveling at the more economical rates take their meals in common mess areas. The food consists mostly of pre-prepared, packaged meals with fresh food made available on occasion. For those with money to spend, restaurants serving freshly cooked meals (or at least above-average pre-prepared meals), are available. Game rooms, observation lounges, studios and computer access rooms are also available to those who pay the necessary user fee. Passengers are free to enter any passenger area not reserved for Business Class or higher.

TRAVELING IN SPACE

► ARRIVAL AND DISEMBARKING

Upon arrival, passengers are once again confined to their cabin or the lounges for the final approach maneuvers. After docking is complete, the stewards and courtesy staff help passengers move their luggage to the arrival customs inspection area. Disembarking passengers are greeted by customs and immigration officers in offices where their documents are checked again. After their luggage is inspected, passengers are allowed entry. Once passengers have cleared customs, they are free to travel to their final destination at their point of arrival.

Travelers must have a medical doctor perform an examination and provide a medical certificate prior to departure, and customs officers will check this document. Passenger service providers will not allow seriously ill persons, or persons with contagious or communicable diseases, passage aboard their vessels, but some people may not develop symptoms until after departure. Any person suffering suspicious symptoms, or that has a suspicious medical history or information present on their medical certificate, is redirected by customs officers for an onsite medical exam. The person is effectively quarantined for the duration of the examination and the time required to return any test data. International treaty does not allow medical quarantine for longer than 72 hours without sufficient medical evidence of danger to the general population. Of course, this has received wide interpretation of the "sufficient" clause.

► CUSTOMS AND IMMIGRATION

Customs and Immigration are two functions that all governments have in place to protect their borders, such as they are. Borders are very subjective, but they are normally defined as any point of entry into the nation from another nation. Therefore, any station, colony cylinder or settlement has a designated entry point where foreign travelers are admitted and subjected to the customs and immigration process. Nations also have a departing customs inspections to ensure that certain products and technologies are not exported illegally, or exported without payment of any taxes or tariffs. Emigration inspections of departing travelers are increasingly common as the cold war between the Jovian Confederation and CEGA heats up. The major reason for this is to prevent military intelligence and other secrets from getting to the enemy. A Customs Officer archetype is located on page 72 in the *Game Resources* chapter under the *Archetypes* section.

The customs officer is a person who performs all the duties of an inspector and bureaucrat. Each traveler and their baggage must be checked by a customs officer. The officer will check the person's identification and background for authenticity. Generally, criminals are not allowed to travel internationally without special permission (although many nations have differing definitions of criminality; political dissidents from the Mars Federation have no trouble gaining entry to the Jovian Confederation, for instance). The person may also be restricted from leaving or entering a nation for any number of other reasons, but this check is meant to prevent any incidents or other complications that may occur as a result of legal limitations. Random baggage inspections are standard procedure, though the customs officer is empowered to perform any inspection they feel has reasonable likelihood of finding contraband items. Generally, any item with a Restricted Class of D or greater is not allowed beyond international borders.

In addition to checking arriving and departing travelers, the customs officer will inspect import and export containers of products and resources, or any other cargo crossing international boundaries. With the present political situation between the various Solar nations, tariffs and duties of various forms are likely to be imposed as a matter of foreign policy. Mandatory checks of all private vessels not following normal schedules are in place as a means to protect national security. Scheduled commercial traffic is also inspected for any number of potential security violations.

⊞ RESTRICTION CLASS

CLASS	DESCRIPTION
A	Illegal to transport, possess, use, sell or store
B	Transportation, possession, use, sale or storage restricted to military organizations
C	Transportation, possession, use, sale or storage restricted to law enforcement
D	Transportation, possession, use, sale or storage of restricted items accessible to civilians
E	Unrestricted

CARGO TRANSPORTATION ◄

Merchant Guild magsail and solar sail ships are the most inexpensive manner of transporting cargo between the planets of the Solar System, but are not the most numerous or timely. Cargo vessels ranging from the smaller Mules to large Cronus-class cargo vessels are also common throughout the Solar System. They can carry virtually any type of cargo between the planets, moons, stations, and colony cylinders. The transport of cargo between the Jovian states on the Hanson Circuit is often reserved for government use, and is fairly expensive for all but the most time-sensitive commercial cargoes. Time-sensitive transportation between other points in the Solar System is normally reserved for optimum orbits and commands the maximum price for services rendered.

Since mass is the all-important arbiter of the cost to move anything around the Solar System, cargo other than passenger travel is based on a per-kilogram formula. The average cost per kilogram for cargo is equal to the square root of the distance between two points in millions of kilometers. This rate is subject to a Cargo Transit Multiplier based upon the type of cargo. Because of the slower transit speed of Merchant Guild sail ships, a final Guild Multiplier of 0.75 is applied.

Gas: Gases are stored in pressurized containers at twenty to thirty atmospheres pressure. A double-hull design with self-sealing membranes ensures that any punctures don't result in catastrophic loss of the gas.

Liquid: Liquids, or liquefied gases, require transportation containers with internal bulkheads to prevent ruptures from shifting loads. The bulkheads are also self-sealing to prevent the loss of liquid if the container is punctured. Loading a liquid container simply requires pumping the liquid into the container. Unloading is accomplished by spinning the container, using centrifugal force and dry inert gas to push the liquid out.

Bulk: Any cargo that has solid form and can be put in a box is classified as bulk cargo. Bulk cargo can range from raw and refined mineral resources to manufactured products of all shapes and sizes.

Secure: Secure cargo is any of the previous cargo types stored in a secured manner. Security can range from special locked and armored containers to various self-destruct mechanisms. In any case, the additional expense per kilogram includes monitoring, the extra weight of the security equipment, and any security personnel required.

Specialty: Specialty cargoes are variations on the three basic cargo types that have unique requirements for transportation. Anything that requires special handling, monitoring, or environmental conditions is classed as specialty cargo. Livestock and artworks are the most commonly-seen specialty cargoes.

CARGO TRANSIT MULTIPLIER ▥

CARGO TYPE	CARGO TRANSIT MULTIPLIER
Gas	x0.1
Liquid	x0.25
Bulk	x0.5
Secure	x0.5 to x2.0
Specialty	x0.5 to x3.0

COMMON IMPORT AND EXPORT GOODS ▥

	IMPORT	EXPORT
Mercury	Food, water	Advanced power technology, shipping services
Venus	Water, biotechnology	Electronics, financial services
Earth	Electronics, complex hydrocarbons, environmental technology	Small arms
Orbitals	Complex hydrocarbons, water	Electronics
Moon	Water, food	Military hardware, light metals
Mars	Nitrogen, complex hydrocarbons	Small arms, environmental technology
Nomads	Food, electronics	Minerals, volatiles
Jupiter	Mineral resources	Electronics, hydrogen fuel, complex hydrocarbons
Saturn	Luxury items, food, space stations	Complex hydrocarbons, volatiles

▶ SPACE NAVIGATION

Real-life space navigation is a complex undertaking, and well beyond what can be incorporated into a roleplaying game. However, space travel is a large part of characters' lives within the **Jovian Chronicles** universe. This section presents a simplified system of space navigation that allows the Players and Gamemaster to help establish what is happening to the Player Characters. Beginning with a simplified explanation of orbits and orbital mechanics, further sections describe how vessels move and relate to other objects within space under this simplified system. A description of space traffic control and the "rules of the road" give Players and Gamemasters an idea of what the people of the Solar System are doing when they direct their vessels between the planets. The section concludes with some discussion on how to use the previous sections with the game itself.

▼ ORBITS AND POSITION

Orbits are described using four conic sections: circle, ellipse, parabola and hyperbola. If the spacecraft's path follows the curve of the orbit, then the focus of the orbit is the center of mass and a source of gravitational influence. The central body — planet, moon, sun or other — is used as a reference point for describing orbits. As orbits change, so can the central body used as the reference point. For example, the planet is used as a reference for orbits about the planet and making the transfer to an interplanetary orbit, but the interplanetary orbit is described relative to the sun. One or more elliptical or hyperbolic arcs define transfer orbits between planets, between orbits or between two points in space.

Planet-synchronous orbits place the craft above a fixed point on the planetary surface. Planet-synchronous orbits are restricted to planets because planets have sufficient gravity to have practical synchronous orbits. For example, a synchronous orbit above the Moon places a vessel in an orbit that would cause it collide with the Earth. Sun-synchronous orbits place the vessel in a fixed orbit with respect to the sun about a planet. For example, Mercurian colony cylinders are in a sun-synchronous orbit that places the cylinders constantly in Mercury's shadow. Polar orbits are perpendicular to equatorial orbits. The major advantage of a polar orbit is the vessel's ability to observe the entire surface of the orbited planet or moon. While this coverage is not complete or constant, the vessel will track across the entire surface area after a number of orbits.

All of these orbits have altitudes described as being low, middle or high. Low orbits are the lowest safe zone in which a vessel can maintain an orbit without spending significant energy to maintain its altitude. High orbits are from a planet-synchronous altitude and higher. Middle orbits fall between low and high orbits. Continuous orbits about planets and moons are either circular or elliptical. Circular orbits place the vessel at a constant altitude, while elliptical orbits vary the altitude from within a few kilometers to thousands of kilometers from a circular orbit. The section on *Flight Rules* details some of the navigation regulations for the orbits described.

⊞ ORBITS AND POSITION

Polar Orbit

Orbital Injection Point

Circular Orbit

Elliptic Orbit

SOME USEFUL TERMS

TERM	DEFINITION
Apoapsis	The point on an orbit furthest from the central body
Periapsis	The point on an orbit closest to the central body
Conjunction	The situation where (or time at which) two bodies are either the same celestial longitude or 180° apart
Eccentricity, *e*	A parameter that defines the shape of a conic section: Circle, *e* = 0; Ellipse, 0 < *e* < 1; Parabola, *e* = 1; Hyperbola, *e* > 1. Eccentricity is a measure of how an orbit deviates from circular. A perfectly circular orbit has an eccentricity of zero; other numbers denote increasingly deviating orbits.
Ecliptic	The plane of the Earth's orbit around the Sun inclined to the Earth's equator by about 23.4°
Injection point	The point at which spacecraft velocity is adequate to enter a planetary orbit
Transfer point	The point at which spacecraft velocity is adequate to move to a new orbit, either planetary or interplanetary
Ascending	Travelling toward the ecliptic from below, or travelling away from the ecliptic from above
Descending	Travelling toward the ecliptic from above, or travelling away from the ecliptic from below
Inclination, *i*	The angle between the orbit plane and the reference plane (usually the ecliptic or the equator of the body)

When a vessel is not orbiting a planet, the simplest method for pinpointing the vessel's position is by the use of polar coordinates. Polar coordinates position a point by the number of degrees from an axis and the distance from the origin. In the case of navigation, the origin is the Sun, and the axis is measured counter-clockwise from a line drawn from the Sun to the Earth's position at the vernal (or Spring) equinox; the axis is 0° celestial longitude. The simplest measure used to denote a third dimension is to refer to the inclination of the plane the vessel is traveling along. The orbit plane, or plane of travel, is the plane defined by any three unique points in the orbit, and is expressed by its inclination relative to the ecliptic. (See *Flight Rules* in the following pages for more information about orbit planes and orbit inclination.) Using a standard ephemeride table that gives a planet's celestial longitude for a certain date, realism-minded Players and Gamemasters can make reasonably accurate guesses about interplanetary orbits and positions.

MOTION, ORIENTATION AND RELATION ▼

Space is a three-dimensional environment that does not lend itself to the usual standards of orientation and motion that are applied on a body with gravity. Motion is defined by the direction and rate of travel. Orientation is direction a vessel is "facing," but it is not the necessarily the same direction as the motion. (For example, to slow itself a ship will turn 180° to fire its engines, thus facing in the direction opposite its motion.) Since both of these quantities are three dimensional, the complexity is greater than required for comfortable game play, so simplification requires reducing the number of dimensions and generalizing actual values by using description. Thus, motion is described in two dimensions; one moves forward and backward along the x-axis, and sideslips left and right along the y-axis. Orientation is described as turning left and right (yaw). One can also turn "up" and "down," with "down" always being the direction of the orbit plane of the nearest reference point. If the unit is facing a target that is not in the same plane, it is assumed to be oriented toward the target unless otherwise noted. The command "New Course" will change the vessel's direction to a new heading.

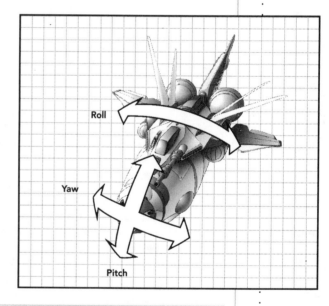

Roll

Yaw

Pitch

MOTION AND ORIENTATION TERMINOLOGY

TERM	DEFINITION
Delta V (velocity)	Describes current velocity of unit
Increase (velocity)	Directive to accelerate to specified velocity on current facing
Decrease (velocity)	Directive to decelerate to specified velocity on current facing
Shift Right/Left	Perform sideslip in the specified direction
Turn Right/Left (degrees)	Directive to perform turn to the specified heading
Delta Plus	Describes the position of a target: the target is accelerating
Delta Minus	Describes the position of a target: the target is decelerating

TRAVELING IN SPACE

◇ RELATION

Relation is the position and motion of the observed (i.e. the target) relative to the position of the observer. (see the diagram at the bottom of the page: the Wyvern's position and movement are measured from the Pathfinder's current position; the Pathfinder assumes that it is motionless in relation to the Wyvern.) This information is reported in a number of ways, all of which are listed in the *Relation Terminology* table. In each case, the target's motion is given with respect to the unit observing the contact. It is not necessary for this to always be the case, but if the observer is reporting to another unit regarding the target, it is required to give the target's position and motion in relation to the position of the unit receiving the report. (e.g. if the Pathfinder informs the Valiant about the Wyvern, the position and motion is reported as if the Wyvern's position and motion are reported from the Valiant's own position.)

⊞ RELATION TERMINOLOGY

TERM	DEFINITION
Inbound (velocity)	Contact moving toward the unit at specified velocity in kilometers per second.
Outbound (velocity)	Contact moving away from the unit at specified velocity in kilometers per second.
x by *y*	Gives the distance to the contact in hundreds of kilometers from the unit's position. "Positive *x*" is contact distance in front, and "Negative *x*" is contact distance behind, the unit. "Positive *y*" and "Negative *y*" gives the distance to the right and left, respectively.
Up (distance)	Unit is between the contact and the orbital plane at the specified distance (in hundreds of kilometers) from unit.
Down (distance)	Contact is between the unit and the orbital plane at the specified distance (in hundreds of kilometers) from unit.
Crossing Right/Left	The contact will cross the unit's current heading from the right or left (up or down is also possible).

⊞ EXAMPLES OF TERMINOLOGY USE

REPORT GIVEN	EXPLANATION
"Hostile, 10 by 5 down 2, inbound 20."	A hostile target is 1000 kilometers in front of, 500 kilometers to the right of, and 20 kilometers in the direction of the orbital plane from the unit, and is closing at 20 kilometers per second.
"Increase plus 5, turn right 45."	Unit increases current velocity by 5 kilometers per second, and turns to the right 45° from its current direction.
"New course. Left 10, decrease 25."	New direction of travel is 10° to the left, and velocity is reduced by 25 kilometers per second.

★ USN SPACE NAVIGATION AUTHORITY

HISTORICAL FACTS

The United Solar Nations Space Navigation Authority (simply referred to as SpaceNav) is descended from the old Earth International Space Traffic Control Office. SpaceNav is responsible for devising and maintaining navigational standards throughout the Solar System. While the space traffic control systems of individual nations differ slightly in their implementation and operation, there are common standards set by SpaceNav to ensure timely, accurate and safe passage of all vessels. Navigation terminology, flight plans, orientation and vector data, flight rules (the "rules of the road"), flight recorder data and systems and navigation communication protocols all follow standards set by SpaceNav. The Space Navigation Authority is also responsible for maintaining central databases for all flight plans and lost vessels, and the placement and maintenance of navigational beacons in specific Solar orbits. The Solar Cross has a close relationship with SpaceNav, with special database access for the purposes of rendering timely humanitarian assistance.

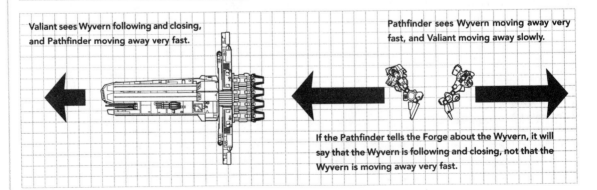

Valiant sees Wyvern following and closing, and Pathfinder moving away very fast.

Pathfinder sees Wyvern moving away very fast, and Valiant moving away slowly.

If the Pathfinder tells the Forge about the Wyvern, it will say that the Wyvern is following and closing, not that the Wyvern is moving away very fast.

FLIGHT RULES ◄

Flight rules refer to the standardized procedures laid out by the Space Navigation Authority for the movement of vessels through space. The latest version of the *Rules and Procedures for Space Navigation* (a.k.a. "the Rules") is over 500 pages in length. Not only does it cover all the flight rules, but also recommends best practices for calculating orbits and maneuvers, and safe piloting methods. Major sections within the Rules specify proper orientation, passing and intersecting orbit procedures, docking procedures, communication protocols and flight plans. The following sections include information about the most commonly used aspects of the Rules.

RIGHT-OF-WAY ◇

Right-of-way is the precedence given to a particular vessel or structure when navigating a course through space. Precedence is based upon the relative mobility of the class of the vessel or structure. Practically, this means that a vessel or structure with high mobility must yield to vessels and structures that are less mobile; in game terms, vessels or structures with higher Maneuver Ratings must yield to vessels or structures with lower Maneuver Ratings. If two ships or structures have similar maneuverability, the larger of the two (based on mass) has right-of-way.

The minimum safe distance between ships mandated by the Rules is five kilometers. A flyby at a distance of five to two kilometers is considered a "near miss," and will result in a warning, and possibly a fine of up to 20,000 credits, to the navigator or pilot of the vessel that failed to yield the right-of-way. A flyby at a distance of less than two kilometers is considered a "near collision," and will result in possible suspension of license and/or a fine of up to 50,000 credits.

OPEN SPACE TRAFFIC ◇

SpaceNav regulations require all vessels in open space to travel close to the orbital plane of their destination. (e.g. vessels destined for Mars must travel approximately within Mars' orbital plane.) Outbound vessels travel below the destination's orbital plane while inbound vessels travel above the destination's orbital plane. Automated beacons are located along different orbits within the orbital plane of each planet to act as navigational reference points.

ORBITAL INCLINATIONS* ▯

Mercury	7.0˚	Venus	3.4˚	Earth	0.0˚
Mars	1.9˚	Jupiter	1.3˚	Saturn	2.5˚
Uranus	0.8˚	Neptune	1.8˚	Pluto	17.2˚
Asteroid Ceres	10.6˚	Asteroid Pallas	34.8˚	Asteroid Vesta	7.1˚

* Measured from the Ecliptic

PLANETARY TRAFFIC ◇

Planetary traffic is defined as vessels moving into, out of, or within a space traffic control zone. Prior to their entry into an STC zone, vessels are required to notify the STC center of their arrival. All vessels entering planetary STC zones perform orbital insertion into high polar orbits before being directed to lower orbits by controllers. Vessels are required to follow the instructions of the STC controllers: while the filed flight plan will give the vessel's orbital insertion data, the controllers may designate new orbits based on traffic and the vessel's final destination within the zone. Automated beacons located throughout the STC zones act as sensor platforms for the entire system, and are also bearing markers for directing traffic.

Vessels performing gravity whips or aerobraking are given priority clearance, provided the maneuver is indicated on the vessel's flight plan. Military vessels are given priority clearance for these maneuvers automatically, though they must still notify the STC center to ensure orbit conflicts are resolved. Vessels may request permission to perform these maneuvers even if the maneuver is not indicated on the flight plan, but must be prepared to receive a less than ideal orbit, risking the need to burn more reaction mass.

TRAVELING IN SPACE

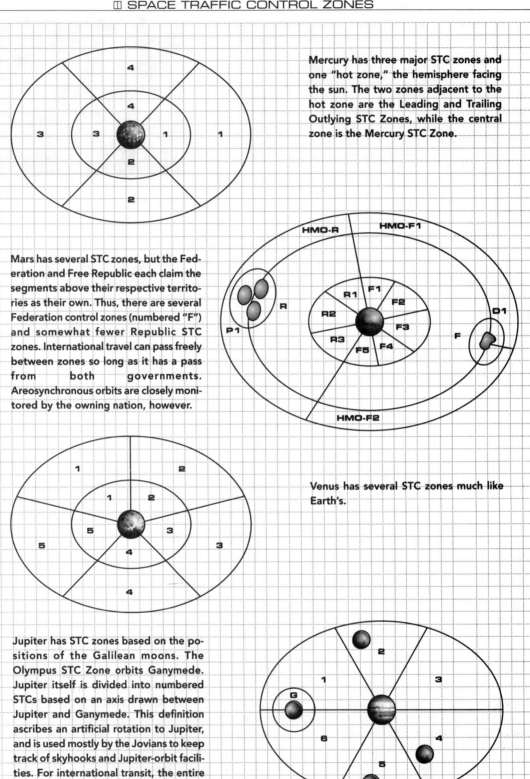

Mercury has three major STC zones and one "hot zone," the hemisphere facing the sun. The two zones adjacent to the hot zone are the Leading and Trailing Outlying STC Zones, while the central zone is the Mercury STC Zone.

Mars has several STC zones, but the Federation and Free Republic each claim the segments above their respective territories as their own. Thus, there are several Federation control zones (numbered "F") and somewhat fewer Republic STC zones. International travel can pass freely between zones so long as it has a pass from both governments. Areosynchronous orbits are closely monitored by the owning nation, however.

Venus has several STC zones much like Earth's.

Jupiter has STC zones based on the positions of the Galilean moons. The Olympus STC Zone orbits Ganymede. Jupiter itself is divided into numbered STCs based on an axis drawn between Jupiter and Ganymede. This definition ascribes an artificial rotation to Jupiter, and is used mostly by the Jovians to keep track of skyhooks and Jupiter-orbit facilities. For international transit, the entire planet is considered one large STC Zone.

LOCAL CONTROL ZONES ★

Local control zones (LCZ) exist within local STC zones around large structures: colony cylinders, stations, autofacs, cargo yards and shipyards. The typical local control is a sphere 50 kilometers in diameter around the structure. With the increased traffic common to the busiest spaceports, the LCZ is sometimes increased to a larger sphere 100 kilometers in diameter. Inhabited moons typically have a local control zone equal to the moon's radius from horizon to horizon, centered on the habitat. To enter the local control zone, vessels must contact the LCZ control center for permission, approach vectors and docking assignments. If a vessel enters the LCZ without permission, it could be assigned a fine (up to 50,000 credits) or suspension of docking privileges.

RESTRICTED SPACE ◇

Restricted space is an area forbidden to unauthorized vessels. There are several possible reasons for restricting an area of space, the primary one being military. The exclusion of prying eyes is the number one reason the military uses for setting restricted areas, be it for prototype testing or war games. Another reason for restricted zones is protection, whether to protect something in the area or the ships that might enter the area. Sensitive scientific experiments, dangerous natural occurrences, or other non-military re-stricted areas are generally set up by government agencies for public protection. Consequences for vio-lating restricted space vary widely and include fines, detention, confiscation or even destruction of the offending vessel. No passage into restricted space is permitted without authorization, and evading detec-tion is unlikely without taking extreme precautions. Those that do have authorization must still follow the normal rules of space navigation.

NAVIGATION LIEN ⊡

A lien is defined as "the right to hold another person's property until a debt on it is paid," and such is the case with a navigation lien when applied to spacefaring vessels. The transient nature of commercial and private vessels means that collecting debts on cargo, services performed (or not), or the vessel itself, is extremely difficult and expensive to undertake actively. A navigation lien against a vessel restricts it from lawfully entering or exiting any STC zone without advancing a minimum fee toward payment of the debt. If the vessel declares an emergency, it is allowed to enter and seek assistance, including docking, but may not leave without paying the fee, nor may it load or unload any cargo (false declaration of an emergency results in a 1,000,000 credit fine). Personnel are not restricted to remain on the vessel, so long as the vessel itself stays out of the STC. Intentional violation of these navigation restrictions (including the false declaration of an emergency) is considered de facto consent to submit to binding arbitration in the matter. The vessel is then effectively impounded until the arbitrator rules.

FLIGHT PLANS ▼

Flight plans are an important part of maintaining the safety of man and machine in space. Though space is very empty, collisions and various accidents can still lead to disaster. The primary reason for requiring flight plans is to double-check all navigation calculations. While navigators diligently check and re-check naviga-tional data, a final check by an independent source ensures that mistakes are corrected early. Second, the flight plan allows STC computers to verify that no conflicts for orbital space are encountered. When close to a planetary body, a vessel cannot see what is on the other side, so potential conflicts are avoided. (Filing a flight plan requires working communications to transmit a copy to an STC center; a copy may be delivered by hand if the vessel is docked at a facility, but departure permission is often denied to vessels without SpaceNav-approved communications systems.)

FLIGHT PLAN INFORMATION ⊡

FILING INFORMATION	VESSEL INFORMATION	FLIGHT INFORMATION	MANEUVERS LIST
Navigator's Name	Name	Departing From	Date/Time*
Navigator License Number	Registration Number	Departure Date/Time	Description*
Filing Date	Transponder Code	Departure Orbit	
	Captain's Name	Arriving At	*for each maneuver
	Number of Crew	Arrival Date/Time	
	Number of Passengers	Arrival Orbit	

TRAVELING IN SPACE

▼ USING THE SPACE NAVIGATION SKILL

Now that we have new information about navigating the Solar System, how can players and Gamemasters use navigation in a game? First, only spontaneous maneuvers require the Space Pilot Skill. Planned maneuvers are entered into the vessel's flight computer, which applies thrust as required, without further human intervention. Properly generating and entering a flight plan is the job of the navigator, and uses the Space Navigation skill. If a vessel's navigator is a Non-Player Character, the Gamemaster is responsible for describing the flight plan, and deciding whether to make any Skill Tests. If the vessel's navigator is a Player Character, the Player controlling the navigator PC should handle navigation. What follows is one possible procedure for roleplaying such a situation.

The Player is responsible for writing out the vessel's flight plans and should follow the example on the previous pages. The only section required is the list of maneuvers. The Player Character's Navigation Skill is tested against the Threshold of each maneuver in the flight plan to determine whether the maneuver is successful. If the flight plan was filed with a space traffic control center for verification and confirmation prior to its execution, the Skill Test for each maneuver receives a +2 bonus. If the flight plan was verified, any Fumbles are treated as Margin of Success 0 (an error or conflict was found and corrected, but not optimized). The magnitude of the Margin of Success, or Margin of Failure, is an indicator of how efficiently and accurately, or inefficiently and inaccurately, the maneuver was conducted. For instance, an MoS of 2 indicates success with a couple of course corrections required, but an MoF of 2 indicates that the maneuver was not quite successful and will require another maneuver to make corrections. A Fumble without STC verification is a serious matter that could possibly put the vessel in danger of collision, atmospheric drag effects, or a highly unstable orbit — whatever works out better for the adventure at the GM's call.

Whether or not the Player or Gamemaster rolls the Skill Test is the GM's decision. The following guidelines can be applied to Skill Tests and Thresholds to ensure a fair resolution of maneuvers. In general, relatively high (twice or greater) or low velocities (half or less) compared to the target body will modify the Threshold by +2 when establishing an orbit. In situations where the maneuverability of the vessel might make a difference, also apply half the vessel's Maneuver Rating (round toward zero) as a bonus or penalty to the Skill Test. If the vessel's engines are damaged, the resulting Maneuver modifier must be applied. A navigator can increase the chances of success by running simulations to check his results. For each simulation run prior to executing the maneuver apply a +1 bonus. Each simulation takes 15 minutes to complete per point of Threshold.

▥ MANEUVER THRESHOLDS

MANEUVER	THRESHOLD
Insertion into orbit	(1 + Vessel's Velocity) / 10, rounded up
Planetary transfer	3
Modify current orbital altitude	2
Modify current orbital inclination	2
New altitude and inclination	3
Gravity-assist	*
Aerobraking	3†

* Details in the **Jovian Chronicles Companion**, pages 86-87.

†Threshold for plotting course only; apply MoS as a bonus, or MoF as penalty, to Piloting Skill Roll. See **Jovian Chronicles Companion**, pages 86-87.

▥ THRUST REQUIRED FOR MANEUVER

Maneuver	Thrust Formula*
Insertion into orbit	[Body's orbital velocity - Vessel's velocity] x d6 (non-negative value; minimum 1)
Planetary transfer	[Body's orbital velocity x Body's gravity x d6] ÷ 2
Increase orbital altitude	Body's gravity x Vessel's Size x d6
Decrease orbital altitude	Vessel's Size x d6
Modify current orbital inclination	Vessel's Size x d6

* Must be applied over successive turns if vessel's Thrust is less than required amount. Modify d6 roll by Navigation Test MoS (subtract) or MoF (add); minimum modified roll result of 1.

SEARCH AND RESCUE ◀

Interplanetary space is huge region that can easily swallow the unfortunate for decades before they are found. There are a number of precautions that are taken both prior and during space travel that help increase the chances of rescue if something does go wrong. The first is the filing of a proper flight plan (see page 35) with the local space traffic control center. This gives searchers some idea of where to start looking for a vessel if something happens. The second precaution is to provide position, course and status updates in regularly scheduled communications with other vessels and automated navigation beacons. Since communication systems keep the previous 72 hours of message traffic in a recording loop, searchers can use this information to shorten their search by beginning at the missing vessel's last known location. The final precaution is to ensure that the vessel is properly maintained, especially its safety systems.

THE SEARCH ▼

Once a vessel misses making regular communications, is overdue without notification, or declares an emergency via radio, the vessel is declared missing. If there are other vessels in the area the missing vessel was last reported, they are required by international law to perform active sensor sweeps of their local area and attempt to re-establish communications. Any debris or other evidence of the missing vessel's possible location or condition is transmitted on open frequencies and to the Solar Cross. Once dedicated search and rescue (SAR) vessels arrive (like the Salvation II-class and Geneva-class ships that perform long circuits through common orbits), they begin by following any reported evidence. Since momentum will carry a missing vessel in the general direction of its last known course, SAR vessels will attempt to catch up to the vessel's projected course before widening the search area. The typical search pattern is a corkscrew that places the search vessel in the space adjacent to the progression of the original course; the corkscrew is gradually widened if there is evidence the missing ship is off-course. Multiple search vessels increase the area covered by running parallel search patterns to cover a larger volume of space. Rescue vessels will often carry surplus exo-armors (with weapons and armor removed in favor of upgraded sensors and more reaction mass) to conduct search and recovery operations.

A major part of locating a missing vessel is detecting the signal from the vessel's Emergency Location Transmitter (ELT). An ELT (Comm +1, range 2000 km, operating duration 48 hours) is installed on all vessels, and contains an independent power supply, system status monitor, navigational computer with related sensors and a transmitter. Large vessels will often incorporate a separate ELT in each major component as backups. The ELT can be activated manually, or it will activate itself automatically in the case of major system malfunctions. As a secondary function, the ELT has a 24-hour memory loop that records critical system information that it will transmit to inform search and rescue crews of the vessel's status.

THE RESCUE ▼

The first priority of the rescue crews is to assess the condition of the target vessel and stabilize it. This task is the most important, since endangering the lives of the rescue crews only makes the situation worse by making it necessary to rescue the rescuers. Most search and rescue technicians (see *Archetypes*, page 69) have some technical training to deal with these situations, but SAR crews also include dedicated technical personnel for stabilizing vessels in distress. While rescue crews are dealing with the crippled vessel, additional craft conduct sweeps to recover any missing emergency life boats and escape pods.

The next step of the rescue is to locate a suitable access point. Airlocks are the preferred point of access, but the SAR crews have other options available depending on the situation. Modified Piranha assault pods (**Space Equipment Handbook**, page 46) are sometimes used to board and evacuate vessels. These are equipped with a detachable airlock that is left on the hull after the crew manually cuts through the vessel's hull; the SAR pod can then make multiple trips to this point to shuttle victims off the vessel.

Once the SAR crews have gained access to the vessel, rescue crews will locate and remove any survivors; failing that, the crews will remove any bodies. This stage also requires the crews to proceed with caution, since exterior inspections seldom reveal interior conditions. It may be necessary for the rescue crews to conduct some repairs to stabilize the vessel before proceeding with a search for survivors. (Refer to pages 45 and 46 in the **Space Equipment Handbook** for search and rescue equipment.)

3.3.1

3.3.2

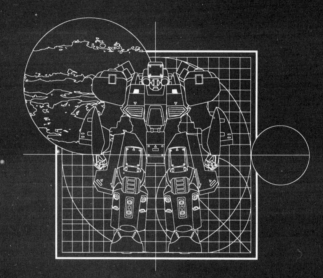

Even though the human race has moved beyond the need to
have solid ground beneath its feet, most of the jobs that
need to be done were done on the ground first. That won't
change anytime soon.
— Otto Kurtz

COMMERCE ◄

Even as the colonies of Earth struggled to survive and become self-sufficient during the years following the Fall, commerce and trade eased some of the hardship, and eventually reunited the newborn nations of the Solar System. Today, commerce in all forms is rapidly expanding despite the political climate. The flow of natural resources has never been greater, as nations build new infrastructures to support and house their populations. Military spending is now higher than at any time in the past century. Between the antagonists, trade has become another battleground to fight upon. Power and money have remained two of the strongest forces driving human actions.

No matter how self-sufficient the former colonies of Earth become, however, they are still very much dependent on commercial activities to maintain and expand their positions. A nation like the Jovian Confederation can perform most of its trade internally without too much worry about the rest of the Solar System, but it can save costs and manpower by trading its wealth of fuel gases for rarer items and services. The neutrality of the Mercurian Merchant Guild establishes their continued presence throughout the Solar System as the quintessential traders of anything; without international trade, the Mercurian nation would likely crumble. The financial giants of Venus are dependent on the continued growth and interconnection of the Solar economies. Earth is struggling to simply supply itself, having suffered greatly during the Fall, and the Orbitals and the Moon hope to become strong enough to survive if CEGA proves to be less than stable in the years to come. Finally, the nations of Mars fight each other economically when not engaged militarily, trying to get the upper hand. This situation has cooled somewhat, but the tensions will remain for many years.

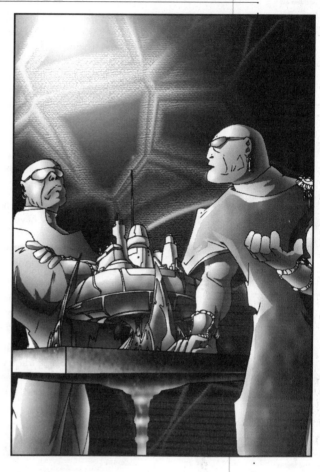

MONEY AND PERSONAL IDENTIFICATION ▼

The credit, issued by the USN's Unified Monetary Council, is the standard system-wide currency. Credit bills are printed on a special green polymer fiber with a tamper-proof holographic serial number and a watermark depicting the people and events of human history. Every eight years the UMC issues a new series of bills with a new historical theme (with the old bill remaining in circulation). The bills come in 1, 10, 100 and 1000-credit denominations. Centicredits are not issued as physical currency, so the standard practice is to round off prices to the nearest full credit.

Many commercial transactions occur electronically as credit card or electronic fund transfers. Electronic transfers involve one party authorizing a financial institution to move money between accounts. Part of the security for fund transfers is to have the two parties, or their representatives, present to transfer funds, or to set a schedule for the transfer of funds. Credit cards incorporate two anti-counterfeiting and security measures: a random (but identifiable) DNA fragment from the user and a thumbprint scan (thumbprint scans are standard security for many different situations). Greater security is provided by retinal, palm, or full-body biometric scans. Accurate and secure personal identification systems are a critical link in the 23rd century. These systems are required for commerce, access to services and use of some personal items. Since much of the business in the Solar System is conducted with electronic funds, personal identification and bank security systems are closely intertwined. The regulations for ensuring the security of an individual's personal and financial information are very strict.

The standard identification also incorporates a personal credit card. The card is a three-millimeter-thick wafer of plastic twelve centimeters long and six centimeters wide. The face has a thumbscan/DNA sampler sensor on one end and a touch-screen display that covers the remainder of the face. A hardcopy of the owner's personal information and a holographic photograph are embedded on the opposite side.

▼ NATIONAL CURRENCIES

Despite the existence of the credit as the standard Solar-System-wide monetary unit, individual nations still issue their own currency for various reasons. The biggest reason for maintaining a national currency is for control over the nation's economy. The second is to provide some protection against manipulation of the unified currency by other nations and the USN; many nations worry about the implications of the USN controlling their nation through controls on the flow of credits to the nation's economy and enemies. At the same time, the use of the credit has helped to stimulate and maintain international trade. There always seems to be a need for something somewhere in the Solar System, and the exchange of these items is facilitated by the credit.

The Non-Aligned States have a variety of currencies for their own use, but deal in credits when conducting business internationally. CEGA officials have protested on a numerous occasions the USN Monetary Council's valuation of NAS currency for USN credits. These protests have been largely ignored since most of the other Solar nations have some trade relations with the NAS.

The Mercurian Ration Point is not an openly traded currency. Only members of the Mercurian Merchant Credit Union (see below) have the ability to exchange Ration Points for other currencies, and vice versa. It is intended and used for internal trade only. With all the international trade the Merchant Guild conducts, the Mercurians have a large amount of foreign currency flowing into Mercury, which is then converted to credits and issued internally as Ration Points.

Lunar cities use the CEGA dollar because of the close relation of the lunar economy to the CEGA Navy. Many Navy personnel take shore leave on the moon, and since they are paid in CEGA currency, the businesses that serve them must accommodate them. Major defense industries that have CEGA Navy contracts are paid with CEGA dollars and thus pay their employees with that currency.

Belt settlements that have aligned themselves with a foreign nation often use that nation's currency internally and for conducting trade with that nation. Neutral settlements will use credits when absolutely necessary, but they prefer to barter for goods and services. THC's Saturn facilities use the Jovian franc since THC is a Jovian corporation, but this is slowly changing to credits as the amount of international trade with Titan increases.

▣ NATIONAL CURRENCY

LOCATION	CURRENCY	LOCATION	CURRENCY
Mercury	Ration Point (arp)	Venus	Yen (¥)
CEGA	Dollar ($)	Orbitals	SHARE (oS)
Moon	Dollar ($)	Mars Federation	Mark (FM)
Mars Republic	Mark (RM)	Jovian Confederation	Franc (Fr)

▣ CURRENCY EXCHANGE RATES

	Credit	Ration Point	Yen	Dollar	SHARE	Fed Mark	Rep Mark	Franc
Credit	-	0.45	0.61	1.30	0.95	1.15	1.20	0.68
Ration Point	2.23	-	1.36	2.90	2.12	2.56	2.69	1.51
Yen	1.64	0.74	-	2.13	1.56	1.89	1.98	1.11
Dollar	0.77	0.35	0.47	-	0.73	0.89	0.93	0.52
SHARE	1.05	0.47	0.64	1.36	-	1.21	1.27	0.71
Fed Mark	0.87	0.39	0.53	1.13	0.83	-	1.05	0.59
Rep Mark	0.83	0.37	0.51	1.08	0.79	0.95	-	0.56
Franc	1.48	0.66	0.90	1.92	1.41	1.70	1.78	-

Note: A singular-valued note of the currency on the left buys the equivalent value of the currency along the top. For example, 1 Dollar is equivalent to 0.89 Federation Marks.

FINANCIAL INSTITUTIONS ▼

"Money, not gravity, makes the planets go 'round," as an old business proverb says. There are financial institutions located throughout the Solar System, but not many are of a scale that can affect national economies, or finance the largest projects undertaken in the Solar System. Each nation has its own national bank that sets the nation's currency policy, interest rates, and other financial functions as dictated by the economy and government policy.

MERCURIAN MERCHANT CREDIT UNION ◇

Given the suspicion that Mercurians have of the Venusian Bank, the Mercurian Merchant Credit Union was formed to provide the nation with financial services. Along with their service on a Guild vessel, Mercurian citizens receive a single share in the MMCU that entitles them to fully access MMCU services. Until they have begun their service requirement and receive their share, Mercurian citizens are only allowed to use the most basic services of the bank. Only Mercurian citizens with MMCU shares can purchase further shares. This arrangement is meant to ensure that the Venusian banks cannot in any way directly influence the Mercurian system. As a result, the MMCU also acts as an economic instrument of the Mercurian administration.

JOVIAN BANK OF COMMERCE ◇

The Jovian Bank of Commerce (stock symbol JVBC) offers its services throughout the Solar System, with the obvious exception of Earth. The majority of the Jovian Bank of Commerce's clients reside within the Confederation, but that has been changing in recent years with increasing rumors and accusations about the activities of the Venusian Bank. Because Jovian Bank of Commerce is one of the few large international banks, they have attracted worried Venusian Bank customers for their stability and the perceived power of the Jovian Confederation.

UNITED SOLAR NATIONS TREASURY BANK ◇

The USN Treasury Bank deals exclusively with currencies and financing multi-national public and private projects. The Treasury Bank comes under the control of the USN Unified Monetary Council, and as such issues USN credits into the Solar economy as directed by the UMC. The Treasury Bank was struck by a financial crisis when the Mars elevator was destroyed, since it was one of the lending institutions responsible for a large portion of the space elevator's financing. The loss taken during the disaster placed a severe strain on the bank's ability to issue new loans, though insurance policies on the elevator covered a fair portion of the loss.

CONFEDERATED BANK OF MARS ◇

Despite the civil war that has split Mars, the Confederated Bank of Mars (stock symbol CBMr) has remained an impartial institution, much like United Martian Delivery Services. Formed from several pre-civil war banking institutions, the Confederated Bank of Mars ensures that Martian interests are served in the best possible manner in both states. Though each nation has a central bank for modifying the national economy, the CBM has strict controls in place to ensure that what happens in one nation does not impact the other. This policy of neutrality has been a burden on the bank, but it has prospered nonetheless.

The Confederated Bank was also hard hit by the destruction of the Mars space elevator. While it recovered some of the capital lost in the disaster through insurance, the bank's stock tumbled sharply before trading was halted. Several private investors purchased minority shares of the troubled bank, and brought it back from the brink. It is strongly suspected by many financial analysts that the private investors are a front for the Venusian Bank.

VENTURE CAPITAL BANK OF VENUS ◇

The Venture Capital Bank of Venus (stock symbol VCB-V) is, essentially, a ghost company for the Venusian Bank. The bank is a completely separate entity from the Venusian Bank, but VCB-V's Board of Directors is completely allied with the Venusian Bank. The statement "it is easier to control the Solar System if you own the Solar System," sums up the intent of the Venture Capital Bank of Venus. By investing in various projects across the Solar System, the Venusians continue to extend their influence through the manipulation of these projects, which includes causing the failure or growth of ventures.

▼ EXCHANGES

Markets exist to facilitate the transaction of goods, services and capital. The capital funds raised by corporations through stock issues sold on the stock markets build colony cylinders and vessels, harvest and process resources, manufacture consumer products and finance technological breakthroughs. By the middle of the 21st century, globalization led to the integration of the world's major exchanges into a single exchange operating around the clock. The physical distances, and the associated communications time delay, separates the exchanges of the 23rd century once again. This regionalization has also led to specialization by region. The exchange regions are Mercury, Venus, Earth (surface only), Orbital/Moon, Mars and Jupiter.

The existence of separate exchange regions gives rise to new regulations concerning the trading of stocks and commodities. For stock exchanges, there are two major rules that govern the trading. The first rule is that a company must have at least ten percent of its operating assets located in an exchange region to trade on exchanges in that region, with each region trading under a separate stock issue proportional to the total operating assets in the region. Second, the company assumes all risk involved with trading in multiple regions. Thus, if the stock price in one region climbs while it falls in another, the company must accept any losses, even if the climbing stock plummets on the news of conditions on another exchange. For commodity exchanges, there is but one major rule: contracts may only be traded in the region of production. Therefore, contracts of Jupiter fuel hydrogen may only be traded on Jovian commodity exchanges.

◇ STOCK EXCHANGES

There are several noteworthy stock exchanges located within the various trade regions. Because of the international exchange rules, most companies trade on a single exchange, or form strategic alliances with complementary operations in another exchange region. Not surprisingly, the largest stock exchange in the Solar System is located in the Jovian Confederation. The combination of being rich in resources and having a strong industrial infrastructure means that a lot of business is done within the Confederation by both local and international companies. Orbital stock exchanges deal heavily in technology companies that are engaged in manufacturing, and research and development. Venus is unique in that it provides another exception to rules regarding exchanges; because of the vast financial resources and services offered by various Venusian corporations, Venus is home to a large venture capital exchange that exists for the sole purpose of helping to raise capital for new or expanding businesses. Some people who have tempted fate on this exchange have compared the experience to dealing with loan sharks, but for every complaint there is equal or greater praise for the exchange.

◇ COMMODITY EXCHANGES

Brokers that buy and sell commodity contracts on the commodity exchanges are seeking to obtain resources for the lowest price, or to obtain the highest price for their resource. The purchase of the right contract at the right time by a shrewd broker can save a company millions of credits as supply and demand forces the cost of resources higher. Companies can also generate a large profit by buying contracts low and selling them high.

The Mercurian Merchant Guild maintains the largest commodity exchange in the Solar System within the Mercurian capital, Helios Station. The exchange trades in a wide range of commodities, namely anything carried aboard Guild sailcraft. Since Guild spacecraft are considered to be an extension of Mercurian territory (much like an embassy), many Guild captains will purchase cargo at one port, sell the contract through the Guild exchange, and then move the cargo to its final destination for the additional transportation fees on top of the contract price. With the Merchant Guild moving a large percentage of international trading goods, it was only natural that the exchange develop here. Buyers are also accepting of what might technically be called a violation of primary commodity trade rule due to the convenience of finding whatever one might need or want at a single point.

The largest resource commodity exchange in the Solar System is located in the Jovian state of Olympus. Mineral contracts and organics from the Belt to Saturn cross the boards of this exchange. By far, the largest and most numerous contracts are for volatiles and hydrocarbons destined for the inner Solar System. Also, in addition to its large mining operations, the asteroid Vesta is home to a commodity exchange that deals exclusively with independent prospector contracts for asteroid rights and resources from Nomad operations.

MANUFACTURING ▼

Automated factories, or autofacs, are responsible for the majority of manufacturing output in the Solar System. While many of the other processes for supporting life outside the Earth's atmosphere require regular or constant human supervision, autofacs work in an almost completely autonomous fashion. The majority of human involvement involves the setup of the autofac and the movement of raw materials and finished products to and from the autofac. Technicians will occasionally perform maintenance and equipment upgrades, but there is little else to do other than check what might be wrong if the autofac's systems report a problem.

The people that create the templates, build the autofac tools, set up the autofac production lines and maintain the autofacs are highly trained and extremely well-paid individuals — 70,000 credits/year for junior technicians to more than 1,000,000 credits/year for template design engineers. The production lines of an autofac are modular by nature, but the cost of setup, or changeover to a new product, means that only products destined for long term production, or requiring special production methods, are manufactured in autofacs; everything else is produced by traditional automated production, assembly line and hand-assembly methods. Some of the production line tools in an autofac are large and complex enough that they will never be moved, and will only be shut down for heavy maintenance.

Each autofac has a raw materials delivery dock on one end, and a finished-products dock at the other end. Both docks also allow personnel access to the interior for maintenance and setup activities. Since there is no permanent human presence on an autofac, autofac are under zero gravity conditions at all times. This also makes it possible for the installation of large access doors along the exterior of the autofac to move production line equipment into and out of the autofac during setup, heavy maintenance or upgrades. Production lines within the autofac may or may not be self-contained to a single item. In many cases, the lines intersect each other to bring together the constituent parts for final assembly. In the case of autofacs used for processing resources, separate processes are located in different lines that split from a single, common materials feed. The only consistent fact of autofac internal layout is that every autofac will differ, even among autofacs producing the same or similar products.

Autofacs are rated by the maximum and minimum number of production lines it can operate, and by the rate of production per day in kilograms. Thus, a 24/12-5000 autofac can produce up to 5,000 kilograms of product on 12 to 24 production lines. Since each line is producing something different, or different parts for final assembly, the amount of raw materials required to complete the process from one end to the other will vary widely. For example, two items may both be created on a 10/15-8000 autofac using three production lines each, but one product may require 2,000 kilograms of raw materials each day, while the other might require only 1,500 kilograms of raw materials per day. Templates and tools will cost between one hundred to one thousand times the production cost of a single item.

▼ RETAIL STORES

Within each nation there are numerous retail chains that offer items to consumers, but there are no truly international chains. Differences in local suppliers, trade and corporate regulations prevent single corporations from effective operation. There are, however, multi-national conglomerates that control different retail chains in different nations that vary across the spectrum of products offered. Entertainment products and services, electronic hardware and software, clothing, transportation, and a variety of common miscellaneous items are all sold by retail stores. More generally, anything that is widely available and produced in large quantities is sold by medium to large retail stores.

There are also many smaller, independent stores that provide a variety of products and services to the consumer. A majority of these businesses deal in specialty items, but there a few smaller shops that can compete with large retail chains through a combination of price, location and service. The primary reason that many people shop the smaller retailers is the service and quality. Many independent retailers also operate as cooperatives where a few full-time staff sell the items produced by part-time contributors. A wide range of cottage industries also provide clothing and other similar products to retailers on a consignment basis. Overall, the products and services are varied, and fill niche markets not covered by larger retailers.

◇ THE BLACK MARKET

The black market is a term for irregular trade avenues that deal in all sorts of goods from simply unavailable or scarce commercial items to illegal weaponry and technologies. Items that can be legally bought and sold in the open, but that are much scarcer in an area (or were stolen), are the most common items available from pawn shops or the friend of a friend of a friend in an alleyway somewhere. The sale of such items is not always illegal, but the prices paid for such items range anywhere from 50% to 500% of the normal selling price. Anything that is illegal to own or sell without a permit is likely available on the black market; one just has to find the right person.

Anyone involved with buying and selling on the black market is patently paranoid about law enforcement officers. Anything less means a short business life as the police or SolaPol quickly swoop in to haul the offender off to be subjected to varying degrees of punishment, depending on the nature of the materials bought or sold. With the tensions between the superpowers of the Solar System, the black market is awash with illegal weapons of all sorts as arms shipments and other items go missing. This has led to increased efforts by SolaPol and other agencies to stifle the flow of illegal goods to black markets.

◐ LEGALITY

Combining the Restriction Class (*Customs and Immigration*, page 28) of an item with its Violation Level provides a Legality Code. The Violation Level of the Legality Code is set depending on the perceived severity of any unlawful, damaging, or dangerous act that can be committed with the item. While it may seem unnecessary to do so with some apparently benign items, troublemakers can always find ways to cause problems with even simple items. Manufacturing any Class A, B, C, or D restricted item without the permission of the local government is universally illegal. The penalties for unauthorized manufacturing are usually one or two levels above the Violation Level of the item being possessed, bought or sold. Legality and Availability are covered in greater depth in the **Space Equipment Handbook**.

ⅠⅠ VIOLATION LEVEL

VIOLATION LEVEL	PUNISHMENT
Level 0:	No violation
Level 1:	1d6 weeks community service; therapy with personal psychiatrist; repayment of damages; 1d6 months probation
Level 2:	minor fines; 1d6 months community service; extensive therapy with psychiatrist; any combination of above; 1d6 years probation
Level 3:	1d6 months incarceration in rehabilitation center; large fines; charge entered on permanent record
Level 4:	1d6 years incarceration in rehabilitation center; huge fines; charge entered on permanent record
Level 5:	permanent incarceration (25 to 50% chance of parole after 10+1d6 years)
Level 6:	permanent incarceration; no parole; death (if applicable)

WORKING BETWEEN THE PLANETS ◄

The many vessels that travel between the planets conduct trade and warfare between the nations of the Solar System. Most of the people that crew these ships have lived their entire lives without a planetary surface under their feet. It takes a certain kind of person to want to live without gravity for long periods, to live in a small enclosure, to deal closely with the same people day after day, and to undertake the daily repetitive tasks of life aboard ship.

As with any organization, there is a chain of command to pass information and direct the actions of those down the chain. The normal chain of command has the commanding officer at the top. The executive officer reports to the commanding officer, and is in charge of the bridge crew and the department heads, and any miscellaneous personnel not attached to a department. On commercial vessels there are normally only two departments: Engineering and Cargo. Passenger vessels will add a third department, Hospitality, for the stewards and other crew that take care of the passengers. Engineering is responsible for the maintenance of ship, and is directed by an engineer with technicians reporting to him. Ships with larger crews will have an engineer and technicians on each crew shift. The Cargo department is responsible for the loading and unloading the vessel's cargo and supplies. They also take part in any extravehicular activities, in which case they are technically on loan to the Engineering department. Finally, the Hospitality department has lots of different duties that keep them busy with the passengers and crew.

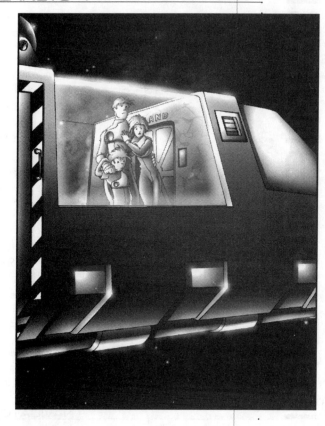

LIFE ABOARD SHIP ▼

Daily life on a ship is really no different than life anywhere else in space. A person's quarters are close to their place of work. All the normal facilities — quarters, mess hall, recreation and entertainment — are available on a ship, but are smaller compared to the same facilities found in larger artificial environments. This gives a person a certain sense of familiarity, even if the difference in scale is very noticeable. Routine is the rule on a ship; certain duties and responsibilities are repeated on a daily basis. It is extremely hard to break the monotony of routine, but most crew members will have their own methods for coping and varying their routine.

Much of the time spent onboard the vessel is spent in the company of others. The close confines of a ship environment quickly teach people how to get along with just about anyone. Anyone who cannot deal with the "flaws" of another person will likely never find work on a vessel again. This close contact also provides an intimacy that draws people to each other. Whether that relationship proceeds beyond casual friendship depends on the persons involved, but romances between the planets are not a rare thing, either. A person's private quarters are considered inviolate; any person disturbing another's solitude, without sufficient reason, may be firmly asked to leave immediately. Repeat offenders are likely have their employment terminated, since a captain can hardly have someone regularly antagonizing the other crew members without it affecting performance.

It is not unheard of for entire families to be part of a ship's crew. Young families are normally only involved in situations where near-constant gravity is available so that their children are not adversely affected. Once the children have become teens, families may venture into new opportunities. Dedicated family quarters are normally only available on larger vessels, but families on smaller vessels will simply occupy smaller, adjacent quarters. Schooling for young children is mostly classroom-oriented, but as they grow, education includes increasing practical experience. The most common result is that the children follow a similar path as their parents after short period of rebellion to help establish something of their own identity.

WORKING IN SPACE

▼ CREW POSITIONS AND DUTIES

The composition of the crew on each ship varies according to its class, and its function. The normal bridge personnel complement includes the captain, first officer, navigator, helmsman and an electronic-emissions specialist. The rest of the crew is usually composed of engineers and a staff of technicians and bosuns. Depending on the function of the vessel, EVA specialists, stewards and any number of possible positions are necessary to operate a vessel. Vessels with smaller crew complements will often combine or overlap positions. (Since military crew positions and duties are detailed in the **Ships of the Fleet** sourcebooks, their duties are not duplicated here. The positions detailed here are strictly from the civilian point of view.)

◇ CAPTAIN & FIRST OFFICER

The captain of a vessel is the person ultimately responsible for everything that happens onboard the ship placed under their care. The conduct of the vessel through space, compliance with international and local regulations, crew safety and actions and the state of the vessel are just some of the many things a captain is occupied with while the vessel is in operation. Since it is not uncommon for the vessel's owner to also be the captain, there are numerous other tasks that are the concern of the captain, such as refits, fuel, cargo rates and all the aspects of running a business. A common career background for a captain is either as a senior bridge crew member or engineering department head, with the former being the most common.

The first officer is responsible for the day-to-day operations of the vessel. The heads of each department report to the first officer, who reports any pertinent information to the captain. The first officer is responsible for finding the right people to fill the various positions aboard the vessel, usually in consultation with department heads. Crew quarter assignments and duty schedules are made by the first officer. When the captain is not present on the bridge, the first officer (or the next most senior bridge crew member) is in command. When docked at a port facility, the first officer must be on the ship if the captain is not on the ship.

◇ NAVIGATOR & HELMSMAN

The navigator and helmsman are not always the same person, but the two positions are very similar and often interchangeable on the smaller ships. Both positions require a thorough knowledge of basic physics and space navigation methods and procedures. In addition to basic course plotting duties, the navigator is responsible for ensuring that flight plans are filed before departure, that said flight plan is respected and that any deviations are reported quickly and efficiently to authorities; the navigator also alters the flight plan as necessary to account for changes in mission or destination. The helmsman is responsible for ensuring that the flight plan is followed, that all necessary maneuvers are carried out in the proper manner, and that all flight systems are operating properly. He carries out the captain's or first officer's flight directives and handles crucial maneuvers such as docking.

◇ ELECTROMAGNETIC EMISSIONS SPECIALIST

The electromagnetic emissions (EME) specialist is the person responsible for operating and maintaining the eyes and ears of a vessel — the sensor and communication systems. On some larger civilian vessels, and on most military vessels, this position is actually divided into two positions that take care of sensors and communications, respectively. The EME specialist is stationed on the bridge of the vessel, ensuring that the space within reach of the vessel's sensors is safe to traverse. The EME specialist also ensures the flow of information between the vessel and the rest of the Solar System. All incoming and outgoing communications traffic must be logged, and possibly checked, to ensure proper use of this vital resource. On smaller vessels where personnel are limited, the EME specialist is also responsible for the maintenance and repair of the vessel's sensor and communication equipment.

EXTRA-VEHICULAR ACTIVITY SPECIALIST & BOSUN ◇

Extra-vehicular activities (EVA) specialists commonly undertake inspections of, and repairs on, a vessel's exterior, or transfer equipment and supplies between vessels. The EVA specialist is trained not only in a specialist field (like a technician), but also to perform in a zero-gravity environment effectively and efficiently. This involves a thorough knowledge of spacesuit use, M-pod operations, airlock operation, numerous safety procedures and the intricacies of moving in zero-gravity.

A bosun is responsible for the maintenance of the vessel's hull and structural framework. Often having cross-training in other technical areas, much of the bosun's time is spent outside the ship inspecting the hull and frame, and patching cracks and abrasions caused by debris and stress. A common part of the bosun's job is also the maintenance of the vessel's point defense systems. Since a lot of the work a bosun performs is exterior, they are experts at EVAs. This means there is a lot of double duty; when not performing their own set of tasks, bosuns and EVA specialists often assist each other.

ENGINEER & TECHNICIAN ◇

An engineer is trained to have a detailed understanding of the vessel's systems as a whole. The majority of an engineer's time is spent monitoring the vessel's plasma chambers and other vital systems. If an engineer is not directly involved with vessel operations, maintenance, repairs, or modifications, the engineer is supervising someone who is involved in such activities.

Technicians are the "mechanics" of a vessel's many systems. Whether the technician is trained to maintain mechanical devices, electrical systems, computer systems, or auxiliary craft, a technician's shift is filled with numerous tasks related to their area of expertise. Given the level of integration between systems, most technicians have some multi-disciplinary training to efficiently carry out their tasks.

SECURITY SPECIALIST & STEWARD ◇

One of the unpleasant facts of living and working in the close confines of a vessel is that small problems can become big problems. The security specialist has numerous duties that involve ensuring the safety of crew, passengers and cargo. More commonly found on vessels with large crews or carrying passengers, the security specialist's primary duty is to enforce discipline. If there is a physical conflict, they are responsible for separating and confining the combatants until the captain takes disciplinary action. The security specialist's training also means he is responsible for coordinating and conducting any defense against someone attempting to board the vessel in open space.

Since the captain or owner of the ship is also responsible for the conduct of their crew, any crew member caught smuggling contraband is not the only one affected by the law should they be caught. The security specialist, therefore, acts on behalf of the rest of the crew to ensure compliance with the laws of any port nation. A law enforcement officer is not always available to investigate a crime that takes place in space, so in such cases, the security specialist will begin the investigation until it is handed over to another agency.

While more common aboard passenger vessels, stewards are also found on other commercial vessels. Small vessels will have crew rotate food preparation duties, or the crew will stock the galley (a small kitchen and mess area) with pre-packaged prepared foods. Larger vessels, with their correspondingly larger crews, will have a steward to prepare meals and coordinate leisure activities for the crew. (For more information, see the Steward archetype on page 74).

WORKING IN SPACE

▶ DOCKING FACILITIES

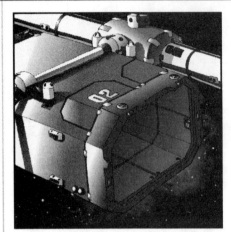

Docking facilities are the ports of call of the 23rd century. Whether the ship is there to deal in passengers or cargo, or overhaul the ship's systems, a stop at a docking facility usually means some downtime for the crew where they can stretch out without worry. As such, most docking facilities have recreation areas where crews can relax in a less confined atmosphere. Passenger facilities commonly include temporary quarters provided by the passenger service if they are waiting to make a connection to another ship, though passenger facilities are usually only a small part of the docking facility's function. Cargo storage is commonly limited to supplies required for facility operations, with dedicated cargo facilities dealing with larger cargo volumes on a daily basis. Maintenance facilities vary from simple parts shops to being capable of conducting full refits. The following section describes the common docking facilities according to their major use.

▼ REFUELING PORTS

Refueling ports, or fuel depots, are usually single, or several, small- to medium-sized asteroids with high volatile content placed into various orbits about the Sun and planets. Also called cyclers, these asteroids carry automated systems that process and store volatiles for future use by a visiting ship. Fuel depots are also created by concurrently mining minerals and removing the volatiles to storage within mined sections of the asteroid. High-traffic orbits will have several cyclers available with multiple fueling stations. A ship requires an access code in addition to the orbital information for the a designated fuel depot. Nomads are frequently contracted to maintain the automated production facilities on these cyclers.

The Jovian Confederation has established the greatest number of fuel depots in the Solar System. In addition to regular shipments of hydrogen to the Trojans from the Jupiter gas mines, the Jovians regularly contract Nomad groups to create roving refueling ports within the large amount of space the Confederation controls. The JAF has numerous refueling ports hidden within the asteroid belt, as do the CEGA Navy and CVNA. Military fuel depots often have stores of munitions and supplies in addition to the fuel stores, so they are often equipped with automated defense systems. Most military depots also have extensive sensor suites for collecting intelligence about local traffic.

▼ SKYHOOKS

Skyhooks are a cheap way of defeating the effects of gravity to move goods between the surface of a planet and space. Instead of extending all the way to the planetary surface, skyhooks are space stations with long tethers that end inside the upper atmosphere to allow jet aircraft to bring items to the end of the skyhook; the cargo is lifted to the transfer station (TranStay) or orbital port (OrPort), and cargo is also brought back down. Cargo is commonly moved to a cargo dock (see below) from the TranStay to minimize low priority traffic around the TranStay since there is limited space around the structure. The orbital port (OrPort) is the most common docking point for ships since it has a higher-velocity orbit compared to the TranStay (i.e. a ship does not need to slow down as much). Refer to **Mechanical Catalog 2**, pages 82 to 87, for more information about skyhooks.

◐ NOMAD SETTLEMENTS

Nomad settlements operate zero gravity docks unless they are located with an asteroid large enough to have its own small amount of gravity. The lack of rotation in many Nomad docks negates the need for any complex maneuvers, thus saving on precious reaction mass. The number of docking stations available will depend on the size of the settlement and the amount of local space traffic. Settlements with a large number of docks act as supply and trade centers for the surrounding settlements, as well as various corporate and independent prospectors and miners. Only permanent settlements have docks capable of being pressurized, so the most common docking station is a simple docking arm. Those settlements with large, pressurized docks often specialize in ship maintenance and refit services that other settlements trade supplies in exchange for.

COLONY CYLINDER DOCKS ▼

All colony cylinders have at least one dock located at the end of the cylinder. This dock can rotate with the rest of the cylinder (thus operating in a low gravity environment), or it can counter-rotate to leave the dock in zero gravity (allowing large ships admission.) Low-gee docks have several smaller doors to allow access to numerous berths within. Zero-gee docks have a large main door with two to four smaller doors around it. Whether a colony cylinder has one or two docks makes little difference to the amount of traffic it handles; the docks are perpetually busy with supplies and people arriving and departing the cylinder. This means the dock doors are rarely closed unless the docks are also closed. All docks are capable of being pressurized, but this rarely done.

Low-gravity docks are most often used for passenger traffic and small cargo transfers, including all regular inter-colony shuttle flights, since the low gravity conditions facilitate faster passenger and cargo transfers. Incoming ships match rotation and enter the dock through the doors. Once the ship is inside, a docking frame is extended to the ship, capturing and withdrawing the ship to a low-gee docking slip. Low-gee docks generally have between 100 and 200 bays of varying sizes.

Zero-gravity docks do not require the use of heavy docking frames to secure ships, so the only true limitation to the size of the ship is whether it fits within the docking bay. A ship is secured with docking arms before personnel access corridors are extended to the ship's airlocks. Zero-gee docks often have external docking arms and access corridors available for ships too big to enter the docking bay.

CARGO DOCKS ▼

Cargo docks are open structures with multiple spines for securing cargo containers until transfer to their next destination. At some point on the perimeter of the dock are attached habitat and hangar modules with offices and equipment for the personnel that operate the dock. The hangar usually has room for six to twelve cargo M-pods. Multiple airlocks are available for personnel in MMUs that work around the dock. An extendible docking arm is also part of the habitat for securing cargo ships. Additional docking arms are located off the end of the container spines. Supply depots are cargo docks that act as cargo storage facilities instead of cargo transfer facilities. (Refer to Yggdrasil-class space station in **Mechanical Catalog 2**, pages 82 to 87, for more information about supply depots.)

A typical cargo yard is constantly loading or unloading cargo vessels, and when there are no vessels to move cargo for, the yard is moving cargo to and from its local destination. Since not every ship needs, wants, or is allowed to dock at the cargo's destination, the cargo yard simplifies the process of cargo delivery. Once the cargo is offloaded, it waits for an OTV to pick it up along with the cargo of other ships. The owner of the yard usually buys the delivery contract from the vessel in question and consolidates the shipments. Managing to run a yard profitably is one of the most difficult business challenges in the Solar System. It is not surprising that these cargo yards are often corrupt, owing their success to a special relationship with a colony dock master or some similar underhanded deal. This technique allows for a much greater flow of cargo and a manageable flow of cargo ships.

SHIPYARDS ▼

A shipyard is either an enclosed structure, or an open framework. An enclosed shipyard is most often used for assembling small vessels, or for refits and major repairs of larger vessels. The enclosed shipyard can operate pressurized or unpressurized, but it is usually only pressurized for jobs taking longer than one month. The largest enclosed yards will have airlocks that can accommodate small vessels and the transfer of large components if the yard is pressurized. Relatively minor repairs are easily accomplished by a ship's crew, but extensive repairs or refits to existing equipment require the ship to dock at a shipyard. Not all shipyards are large, immobile facilities. Ships like the Jovian Armed Forces' Gagarin-class fleet tender and the CEGA Navy's Detroit-class fleet support ship are capable of handling these repairs in the field, being mobile shipyards in their own right.

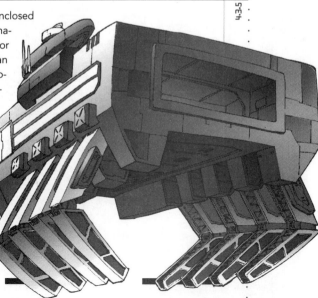

► EXTRA-VEHICULAR ACTIVITY

Extra-vehicular activity (EVA) involves leaving the confines of an artificial environment for a journey across non-Earth landscapes or through the void of space. The two constants of EVAs are spacesuits and airlocks — the first is required for survival and the second is required for access. M-pods are another common component of EVAs around colony cylinders and vessels (where they are used for construction and maintenance), shipyards and cargo docks (where they are used for moving materials), and during travel and exploration trips (where they are used for moving and using large pieces of equipment).

It has long been standard practice to have the atmosphere in space habitats use lower than Earth-normal air pressure. Along with advances in materials and spacesuit design, the user can simply get into a spacesuit and enter an airlock to begin an EVA. (The pure oxygen atmosphere used in 20th and early-21st century suits required the user to pre-breathe oxygen for many hours to avoid decompression sickness.)

There are two safety rules for EVAs that are considered sacred: 1) one should never leave the airlock alone, and 2) someone else must double check one's suit before entering the airlock. While the first is not always possible in some circumstances (requiring extra caution and attention by the person involved), the second rule is never violated except in extreme emergencies.

▼ SPACESUITS

Spacesuits are worn whenever people leave the artificial environment in which they live. Each suit is fitted to the wearer using modular, interlocking pieces: a helmet, torso, arms, gloves, legs, boots and mission pack. It is normal practice to leave the boots attached to the legs and the arms and mission pack attached to the torso, in order to make getting into the spacesuit easier. A control pad is mounted on each forearm. The control pad consists of a small display screen with selection buttons around the perimeter of the screen. A suit systems monitor also reports any internal systems malfunctions.(See the **Space Equipment Handbook**, pages 11 to 18, for more information about spacesuits and their options.) The following table describes the control pad menus with functional descriptions.

▥ SPACESUIT CONTROL PAD MENUS

MAIN MENU	MENUS	BUTTON(S)*	FUNCTION
Control	BodyTemp	Head, Torso, R. Arm, L. Arm, R. Leg, L. Leg, +, -	Set the temperature for different areas of the body
	Gas	+, -	Controls the rate at which the atmosphere is cycled through the suit
	Test	None	Pressure Test; Displays pressure reading and recommendation about suit integrity
Comm	Preset Freq	Select from listed preset frequencies	Press to select a pre-programmed communication frequency
	Select Freq	KHz, MHz, GHz, +, -	Displays current frequency
		Scan	Select any active frequency in the selected band. Press again to skip to the next active frequency.
		Preset	Switches to the Preset Freq screen to select the preset slot for the current frequency
	Mode	PTT	Push to Talk: requires the user to press the PTT button to transmit
		VOX	Voice Activated: transmits everything the user says in a normal voice
		OPEN	Open Channel: transmits everything (open line)
	Hardline	Open, Close	Activates the hardline communication connection using the current Mode
Monitor	Gases	None	Displays minutes left at current rate of consumption
	Radiation	None	Displays current accumulated exposure and rate of exposure
	Body Temp	None	Displays body schematic with relative temperature by color
	Power	None	Displays minutes left at current rate of consumption
	Diagnostics	None	Displays minutes left at current rate of consumption
Hardware	(Body Location)	Variable	Sub-Menus and displays depend upon the installed systems
	MMU	Remass	Displays amount of reaction mass available as numbers of activations remaining
		Enable VOX, Disable VOX	Turn voice commands on and off
Emergency	Beacon	Activate, Deactivate	Press and hold five seconds: turn the suit's emergency locator on and off
	Purge	Yes	Press and hold five seconds: purges the suit's atmosphere and then replaces it
	Reset	Oxygen, Remass, Temp, Rad	Silences and resets alarm
Lock	Lock	None	Press and hold five seconds: lockout control pad functions
	Unlock	None	Press and hold five seconds: restore control pad functions

*Note: Each menu has a button designated as "Previous" to return to the previous menu screen.

USING A SPACESUIT ◇

Before suiting up, the wearer checks the entire suit for physical damage such as tears, punctures, dents or deep scratches. The wearer also checks that the locking rings at the shoulder and ankles have proper seals. The locking rings at the wrist and neck are checked by test-fitting the gloves and helmet. The mission pack has gauges for direct readings of gas, power and coolant gel levels that the wearer can check before using a spacesuit. A supply line is also connected to the mission pack resupply socket to ensure that the mission pack is fully charged. Of course, if there is any damage to the suit, or the gauges are providing incorrect readings, the wearer will deactivate the suit, attach a warning label, and move the suit to a maintenance area.

The main airlocks are usually in an area of low or zero gravity, so the weight of the suit is minimized, making it easy to suit up when alone. Stored in a room next to the airlock, the torso/mission pack are stored in a rack along a wall where the wearer can stand up into the torso and arms. Due to the low gravity, the legs and boots are stored standing up next to the torso rack, so that the wearer can simply lower himself into the lower half. The locking ring at the waist is secured. The helmet is attached next, followed by the gloves.

An overpressure test is available to check for leaks. Using the suit control pad, the user simply chooses the "Control" menu, and then "Test." The suit's internal computer will ask for confirmation; it will then pressurize the suit to 48 kilopascals (14 kilopascals above normal pressure) and wait for two minutes. If the suit's internal pressure does not drop during that time, the suit is properly sealed, and the internal pressure returns to the ambiant one.

AIRLOCKS ▼

An airlock is used as an entrance and exit between a pressurized environment and an unpressurized environment. An airlock door is composed of two sections; one section opens into the airlock while the other opens in the opposite direction. Each door section is wide enough to allow an individual wearing a spacesuit to pass through. This helps prevent depressurization accidents since the sections reinforce each other, plus the opening caused by a section failure is smaller and easier to repair. The airlock door is opened and closed automatically from the controls for that door. There is also manual system recessed within each door section if power fails.

Each door has a set of controls located next to it on both sides. Each set of controls has an indicator panel, pressurization control and a door control. The door control is located on the right side of the airlock door, next to the door section that opens into the airlock. In case of a power failure, the airlock has an independent power supply that runs the indicator lights and pumps. The indicator panel displays the positions of the doors, airlock pressure level, and the operating status of the airlock using colored lights. The lights are solid or flashing red and green, and in one case solid yellow, as noted in the table below.

AIRLOCK CONTROL PANEL ⑪

INDICATOR	COLOR	STATUS
Exterior/Interior	Solid green	Door closed
	Flashing green	Door closing
	Solid red	Door open
	Flashing red	Door opening
Pressure	Solid green	Airlock pressurized
	Flashing green	Pressurizing airlock
	Solid red	Airlock depressurized
	Flashing red	Depressurizing airlock
Status	Solid green	Airlock operating normally
	Solid yellow	Airlock using emergency power
	Solid red	Airlock currently in use

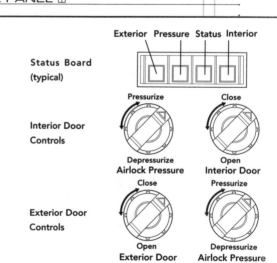

◇ DEPRESSURIZATION SAFETY

Several safeguards are in place to prevent depressurization accidents. The exterior door cannot be opened if the airlock is pressurized, and the interior door cannot be opened if the airlock is depressurized. The airlock will not pressurize if the exterior door is open, nor will it depressurize if the interior door is open. If one door is opened, the second door will not open until the first door is closed; if a door is opened from outside the airlock, the second door will only open from inside the airlock, and vice versa. If an emergency is declared, the airlock will switch to emergency mode and allow override of these safeguards. To do so, the switch is activated at least three times in rapid succession, and then left at the desired operating position.

Within the airlock are resupply and recharge lines for filling mission pack expendables and MMU reaction mass. This allows EVA workers to quickly recharge before returning to work, without having to fully reenter the habitat. Also located within the airlock are emergency spacesuits and survival bubbles. Some airlocks have cradles for storing MMUs. Airlocks regularly used by maintenance or construction workers will also have tools and equipment stored in lockers.

▼ MAINTENANCE PODS

Maintenance pods, or M-pods for short, are large manned maneuvering units with all the options. M-pods have, at minimum, one set of manipulator arms, with the most common configuration being one pair of heavy and one pair of light manipulators. Higher thrust and larger reaction mass reserve allow M-pods to move larger, high mass equipment that would not be efficient to move using MMUs. One of the common uses for M-pods is to maneuver and hold large pieces of equipment for spacesuited workers while they work on or install the equipment. The advanced control system of an M-pod takes into account the change in overall center of mass when moving items. All movement commands are executed according to the center of mass of the M-pod and cargo combined. Each M-Pod is equipped with a heads-up display that provides information about the pod's motion and orientation, the position of the manipulator arms, and objects in close proximity to the pod.

◇ M-POD OPERATION

M-pods are operated in a manner similar to MMUs. (See the **Space Equipment Handbook**, pages 67 to 69, for more information about MMU operation.) Instead of temporary switches like an MMU's controls, the M-pod has a pair of joysticks to control its movement, with the right stick controlling movement along the M-pod's axes and the left controlling rotation about the axes. Numerous buttons and switches on the joysticks can be programmed to accommodate hands-free operation of M-pod systems. Beside the joysticks are waldo gloves; these control the manipulators by mimicking the motion of the pilot's arms. The thumb, index finger and middle finger are used to control fingers and thumb on the manipulator, while the ring and little fingers have access to several programmable buttons.

The controls for MMUs are standardized between every model of MMU manufactured in the Solar System. A temporary switch is tied to each of the six movements that a MMU performs: rotation about the x-axis (roll), y-axis (pitch) and z-axis (yaw), and movement along the x-axis, y-axis, and z-axis. (By default, the left hand controls rotation and the right hand controls translation; however, the user can reverse the movements controlled by each hand.) A failsafe switch is included with the controls to ensure that the MMU does not activate when a switch is unintentionally pressed. The most common control used is a large rocker switch that releases a controlled burst of reaction mass, producing a small fraction of a gee acceleration. The switch must return to the neutral position before another command is activated. This activation method allows for great control since a single burst that starts a motion in one direction is stopped by a single burst in the opposite direction.

⊞ M-POD CONTROLS

JOYSTICK ACTION	RIGHT JOYSTICK	LEFT JOYSTICK
Forward	Movement forward	Pitch down
Rearward	Movement backward	Pitch up
Right	Movement right	Roll right
Left	Movement left	Roll left
Twist Right	Movement up	Yaw right
Twist Left	Movement down	Yaw left

M-POD VOICE COMMANDS ◇

Voice commands are given in a specific sequence of commands with pauses, and no other sequence will activate the system. First, the voice command system is brought to an active state by the spoken word, "Move," informing the system that the movement command and parameters will follow. Since speaking normally opens communication channels, an active voice command system temporarily routes all speech through an internal buffer that filters conversations to avoid accidental activations. The next word spoken is the actual command the MMU will perform. Some commands also require parameter information, following the command word, to function. The *Voice Command* table summarizes each command and its parameters. Parameter options are divided by slashes to indicate the options available; commands with parameters will not function without the proper parameter information. In case a command is misspoken or incorrect, "Cancel" will clear the command sequence queue. Commands are executed one at a time in sequence (i.e. the user can give another command while the M-pod executes the first command sequence in the queue).

The standard commands encompass a variety of control issues that can be very hard to overcome without a great deal of practical experience. "Stabilize" provides the user with a quick and easy way to stop any rotation, especially rotation that results from the use of the manipulators (the user must have already defined a point of reference for the M-Pod's computer). "Stop" is another useful command to quickly arrest the movement caused by outside personnel or manipulator use. Advanced voice commands allow for normal movements with precision control via an inertial navigation control system. Provided the motion command and a motion parameter, the navigation system moves the user as specified. "Translate" moves the user along one of the three axis that defines a direction relative to which direction the user is currently facing. Translation along the "X"-axis moves the user forward ("Plus") and back ("Minus"). Translation along the "Y"-axis moves the user right ("Plus") and left ("Minus"). Translation along the "Z"-axis moves the user up ("Plus") and down ("Minus"). "Rotate" turns the user about one of the three axis. Rotation about the "X"-axis turns the user on their side, turning to the right ("Plus") and left ("Minus"). Rotation about the "Y"-axis rocks the user forward ("Plus") and backward ("Minus"). Rotation about the "Z"-axis spins the user right ("Plus") and left ("Minus"). The "Hold" command cancels any an rotation about, or translation along, a specified axis. The "Rapid" command is used in place of the "Move" command to specify that the MMU carry out the maneuver at quickly as possible, thus consuming reaction mass at quadruple the normal rate (four BP per one MP).

VOICE COMMANDS

COMMAND	ACTION	COMMAND SYNTAX
Move	Prepares system to receive commands	"Move."
Cancel	Clear command sequence queue	"Cancel."
Stabilize	Stops any rotation about axis	"Stabilize."
Stop	Zeroes relative motion along axis	"Stop."
Command	Turn voice command movement on/off	"Command. Activate/Standby/Deactivate."
Translate	Shift along an axis	"Translate. X/Y/Z. Plus/Minus (distance in meters)."
Rotate	Rotate a fixed arc about axis	"Rotate. X/Y/Z. Plus/Minus (number of degrees)."
Hold	Maintain absolute position	"Hold. Lock/Unlock."
Rapid	Perform high energy movement	"Rapid. (Command). (Parameters)."

EXAMPLES OF VOICE COMMANDS

"Move. Translate. X. Plus five."	Moves the user five meters directly forward
"Move. Rotate. Cancel."	System prepares to rotate, but the command is cleared by the user
"Move. Stop."	M-pod brings the user to a complete stop gradually
"Move. Rotate. X. Plus 90."	Rotates right, perpendicular to original orientation, but still facing in the original direction

WORKING IN SPACE

▶ SPACE CONSTRUCTION

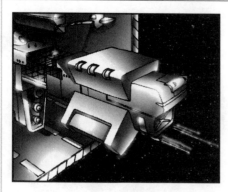

From Humankind's earliest days, it has built all manner of things; this has not changed in the 23rd century. New colony cylinders, stations, ships and habitats are continually under construction throughout the Solar System. Automated factories (see *Manufacturing*, page 43) provide the finished materials and parts to build habitats and ships. In the case of surface structures, finished materials are produced in orbit and brought to the surface, or they are produced on the surface using native materials. To help in the construction of Nomad settlements in the Belt, a consortium of Nomads built and continues to operate a number of mobile autofacs that travel the Belt to produce required materials for Nomad settlements on-site.

▼ COLONY CYLINDER

Colony cylinder construction begins at one end of the structure, usually the end with the stationary (low gravity) docks. The main structural skeleton of the cylinder is the first thing to be assembled. As the skeleton progresses, a follow-up crew begins to install the machinery located between the skeleton members. Following the machinery installation, the outer layers of the cylinders skin are applied. Interior foundation decking and shielding is installed over the skeleton and machinery. Before the far end is capped, thousands of containers are stored within the cylinder to finish the interior. It is common practice to install the raised monorail pathways through the cylinder interior as the cylinder skin is installed. The monorail system is the first fully functional component inside the sealed cylinder, being used to move work crews and materials inside the cylinder. Thermal radiators, communication arrays and life boats are also installed on the surface of the cylinder as the exterior surface is completed. For Vivarium cylinders, the sunline is assembled as the skeleton is almost assembled. Segments of the sunline are produced prior to installation within the cylinder.

Once the main body of the cylinder is completed and sealed, a pressure test is conducted to check for leaks and test the operation of the life support system. After the leak check, the cylinder is brought up to normal pressure so the crews can work without spacesuits. The cylinder is also spun up to produce a low gravity environment to simplify work without requiring all the machinery necessary at normal gravity. Work crews begin by assembling standard living quarters. Once these are assembled, and other supporting structures are built, the construction crews will continue to live within the colony cylinder until the interior is completed. As quadrants of the interior are completed, the citizens of the new cylinder begin moving into the cylinder. This provides additional services to the crew, with the new citizens often spending their free time helping to finish landscaping and other odd jobs within the cylinder.

▼ SHIPBUILDING

A typical shipyard is located near the autofacs that produce the ship components. The components are then delivered to the shipyard for final assembly. Open-framework shipyards are simply structures to support the major components of the ship being built. These yards are used for assembling large components such as the ship's keel, engines and gravity wheels; major bulkheads and hull skins are also assembled in open yards. For ships that are manufactured from modular sections, the open shipyard is used for final assembly of the component modules. Pressurized shipyards assemble smaller ships and modular sections for larger ships. Components and finished ships are brought into the docks through large airlocks.

▼ STATIONS

Space stations are small compared to the enormity of a colony cylinder. Most stations are modular in design to allow for sections to be built at a central shipyard before being moved to their final location. The station is often assembled at the shipyard, whose crew performs systems integration tests and ensures that the final assembly on-site will proceed smoothly (since it would be very inconvenient to tow the section back to the place of manufacture.) Before the station is moved to its final assembly point, the sections are disassembled and filled with supplies, equipment and furnishings to finish the interior outfitting on-site.

SALVAGE ◄

It is a sad fact of life that there is a constant need for people skilled in the recovery of vessels and property from the emptiness of space. Whether the vessel in question is a warship damaged in battle a week ago or a commercial freighter missing for a decade, there are people waiting for the recovery of valuables from the ship itself to the contents thereof. The work of salvage crews is often dangerous, but the rewards are great for those involved in what can be a time-consuming and tedious job.

Every component of most ship or structure in space is marked with a serial number for identification in case of disaster. A detailed database of the components and their serial numbers and which ship or structure they are currently a part of is catalogued, and the current whereabouts and disposition of those items is tracked whether they are in storage or being moved as cargo between two points. The Salvage Office of the USN Space Navigation Authority maintains this database. Salvage operators pay an annual access maintenance fee of 50,000 credits, plus a find fee (1000 credits per search) for database access should they ever happen upon something.

While some salvage operators concentrate almost exclusively on items long missing, other operators are more concerned with recent losses. The military conflicts of recent years have made salvage work very lucrative; the governments involved issue regular contracts, and even commit to secret salvage operations in the hope of retrieving enemy vessels damaged in battle. Depending on the condition of the hulk, the salvage teams can expect to get from 5% (if mostly scrap) to 50% (if largely intact) of the vessel's value. Depending upon the cargo and other miscellaneous items present onboard, the teams could potentially earn many times what the actual ship is worth.

The Solar Convention on Salvage provides some guidelines for setting the value of any compensation due. Under the terms of the Convention, any vessel that has been lost for less than ten years is still the property of its owner(s). In this case, salvage teams will have to contact the owner and ask permission to salvage the vessel if it is abandoned. If the owner does not give permission to salvage, tradition dictates that the owner refund the salvage team their database access fee and pay a gratuity for the lost vessel's location and orbit.

SALVAGE OPERATIONS ▼

Salvage operations are a delicate dance between the recovery craft and the object to be recovered. Combat salvage is even more delicate since the object is often rotating about multiple axes and will likely contain explosive materials. Salvage crews are extremely well-trained and well-equipped for their task. A large part of the salvage teams are EVA specialists who are proficient in numerous technical skills. Many salvage personnel are former shipyard workers, so they have an intimate knowledge of ship systems.

Salvage ships carry many heavy duty M-pods for stabilizing and modifying the orbits of vessels and moving recovered materials and personnel between vessels. Large cargo bays are another common feature of salvage ships, with expectations that they can be filled with salvage. Most salvage ships' computers contain detailed blueprints for known ships for use by the salvage teams in their tasks. Large reserves of reaction mass are carried to shift orbits, to fuel the salvage vessel's many auxiliary craft, and to tow salvage to port. A wide range of tools is carried to ensure efficient conduct of salvage tasks. It is not uncommon for salvage vessels to carry at least one squad of exo-suits for self-defense of the ship and the salvage.

◇ STEP ONE

If the crew believes it has found a lost vessel, the first step is to attempt communication by radio and check for a transponder signal. If there is no response, the crew will move to intercept the vessel and establish visual contact to check for operational navigational lighting. The use of Morse Code to establish communications by flashing the navigation lights is common practice when the radios are damaged. At the same time, the crew will try to match the other vessel's course. The crew also checks the transponder signal (if there is one), or the vessel's registered name on the hull, against the SpaceNav database for lost or missing ships. If the vessel is missing, the salvage vessel will begin rescue operations (which may become salvage operations, depending on the situation). A visual inspection is also carried out to determine the condition of the other vessel; the crew looks for things like missing lifeboats, escape pods and physical damage.

◇ STEP TWO

Once the lost vessel is determined to be salvage (the SpaceNav database returns a positive result, and/or the vessel's owner is contacted), an EVA team will perform a close inspection of the exterior, and also board the vessel for an interior inspection if it is considered safe to do so. The bodies of any remaining crew and passengers are recovered before any salvage is taken. A detailed record of location and condition of any recovered bodies is made for presentation as evidence at potential legal proceedings. After the inspection and removal of bodies is complete, a decision is made as to what method of salvage will be used: scrap, tow, recover, recover and scrap, or recover and tow.

◇ STEP THREE

Once the decision is made about the salvage method, the vessel's flight data recorder (the "black box") and computer core are recovered from the vessel. If the salvage team has a salvage-certified electronics expert onboard, he will make duplicates of the data and transmit a copy of the data to the SpaceNav Incident Investigations Office. The recovery of the black box and computer core is the only salvage task the salvage team is legally obligated to perform. The salvage team then proceeds with the rest of the salvage work.

◇ STEP FOUR

Scrap operations involve quickly removing anything of potential value from the vessel. Equipment is removed, chunks of bulkheads and the hull are cut loose, and cargo containers are offloaded. Tasks are quickly done to minimize the time spent with the vessel. This kind of salvage is often undertaken due to difficult orbits or dangerous circumstances, such as collision courses or intervention by military forces.

Recover operations are much more time-consuming compared to scrap operations. Everything aboard the ship is removed. Personnel effects of the crew are packed (to be returned to the owner's family in expectation of a gratuity payment), subsystems are completely removed, cargo containers are removed and catalogued, and reaction mass is transferred to the salvage vessel. Once this is completed, the hulk will either be towed to a port or scrapped as above.

◇ STEP FIVE

If the vessel is in good condition structurally and operationally, the vessel will likely be towed back to a shipyard for closer inspection, and possibly refit and repair. Depending on how well the salvage team is equipped, Step Four and Five might be reversed so that the team can access additional personnel and equipment for scrap or recovery tasks.

◇ STEP SIX

Once salvage tasks are complete and it is decided that the hulk is not to be towed to port, the hulk will be destroyed by pushing the hulk into a degenerating Solar orbit that will burn the hulk in the sun. If orbital mechanics make this too costly, the hulk will be put into an orbit that sends it out of the Solar System or somewhere else out of the way.

THE SOLAR CONVENTION ON SALVAGE ▼

As Humankind traveled more frequently into space, the inevitable accidents occurred — vessels were lost, and later found. It did not take long before the old Earth International Convention on Salvage was adapted for use beyond Earth's oceans. In 2189, five years after the emergence of CEGA and 200 years after the original maritime version was instituted, the convention was again ratified by the Solar nations as the Solar Convention on Salvage (SCS). The administration of the SCS falls under the mandate of the USN's Space Navigation Authority (SNA).

NOTABLE ARTICLES OF THE CONVENTION ◇

For the sake of brevity and clarity, a brief summary of notable Articles is provided here. A more complete text on the Solar Convention on Salvage is included in the *Game Resources* chapter on page 76.

Article 3 — Platforms

Unmanned or immobile platforms engaged in scientific research, or resource exploration and exploitation are not covered by the convention (i.e. a party cannot salvage an unmanned gas miner).

Article 4 — State-owned Vessels

Vessels owned by the a nation are not subject to the Convention and are entitled to sovereign immunity under international law. The nation may apply the Convention to its vessels, but must notify the SNA Chairperson of the terms and conditions associated with the application of the Convention. This does not mean State vessels cannot be salvaged, but if they are, salvors cannot expect remuneration for their salvage.

Article 9 — Rights of Solar States

The State is allowed to take actions to protect itself from spaceborne threats that supersede the interests of the vessel owners and salvors.

Article 10 — Duty to Render Assistance

Every master is bound to render assistance to any person in danger of being lost in space. Each nation is responsible for ensuring the enforcement of this Article (i.e. setting out criminal penalties for failing to render assistance). The owner of the vessel is not liable for any breach of the Article by the master.

Article 13 — Rights of Salvors and **Article 14 — Special Compensation**

These articles detail the means and levels of compensation due the salvor. Payment due is set under legal contract, and as such the parties involved can take legal actions under these Articles to remedy disagreements about compensation.

Article 16 - Salvage of persons

A person saved from distress is not obligated to compensate his rescuer, but may do so. A rescuer of human lives is entitled to a fair share of the salvage awarded to the salvor for salvaging the vessel.

Article 18 - The effect of salvor's misconduct

Payment may be withheld due to negligence or incompetence in the conduct of the salvor's duties.

Article 25 — State-owned Cargoes and **Article 26 — Humanitarian Cargoes**

The Convention cannot be used as the basis for seizure, arrest or detention of non-commercial State or humanitarian cargoes.

BRIEF GLOSSARY OF TERMS ⅏

TERM	DEFINITION
Master	vessel's commander
Salvor	party conducting salvage operation
State	a sovereign nation
Vessel	any ship or craft, or any structure, capable of navigation

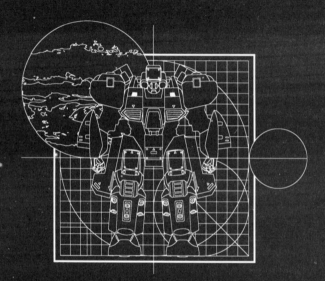

Question: "So what have you been doing today?"
Answer: "Oh, nothing much. Just hanging around."
— Typical low-gee climber humor

SPORTS ◀

When people moved from Earth to the many places they now call home, they took their love of recreational and competitive sport with them. Unfortunately, Earth gravity wasn't always available for Earth sports, so the ingenuity and creativity that helped forge nations in space changed the games they played. Where there is standard (or near-standard) Earth gravity, there are the sports that have been played on the ground for centuries. Since most colony cylinders are at or close to standard gravity, there are facilities to accommodate a wide variety of popular sports that anyone can play.

There are also numerous competitive teams and leagues for just about every popular sport. For those that play sports only casually, equipment rentals are available. Organized amateur and recreational leagues are common throughout the Solar System, since the health benefits provided by physical activity are unmatched, especially for those that live in less than normal gravity. Universities and colleges have maintained the practice of providing scholarships to promising young athletes looking to move into the professional ranks. Professional sports is still big business, though on a smaller scale compared to professional sports during the late 20th and 21st century. Tickets to professional-league games vary in cost between 25 to 200+ credits per game, depending on the seating location and services provided. Tickets for an entire season will normally save the purchaser between 10 and 20 percent compared to single game prices.

LOW-GRAVITY SPORTS ▼

Several sports that are played under normal gravity translate well to low gravity with some modifications, and with what some would call improvements. The power and dexterity brought to low-gravity sport allow for truly spectacular displays of athletic and physical prowess by competitors. While normal-gravity sports are still popular, the sheer spectacle of some low-gravity sports attracts large groups of fans and participants.

Lower gravity has several profound effects on most court sports — volleyball and basketball being the two most popular. The height players can attain and the power they can impart to the ball is immense when compared to competition in normal gravity. The first modification to these two sports is the height of the net or basket. This height increase is proportional to the decrease from normal Earth gravity (i.e. a 50% decrease in gravity results in a 50% increase in height). The courts are normally expanded in size by a similar amount. Volleyball and basketball are usually not played in less than 40% of normal gravity. Most normal-gravity sports have some variation in low gravity, but the variations are not always easily recognizable as being derived from a certain sport. In fact, many low-gravity sports have incorporated elements from multiple sports.

Martial arts as sport has grown steadily in the past two centuries. The coordination and fitness benefits gained by low- and zero-gravity residents through the practice of a martial art are major reasons for the immense popularity. As a spectator sport, martial arts in low gravity are filled with spectacular sequences of moves that are otherwise impossible in normal gravity. Hand-to-hand martial arts are generally the only ones conducted at low gravity unless the participant is already highly accomplished with a weapon at normal gravity. A variety of fighting venue designs are used depending on the combatants' skill and the martial art. Some of the most popular venues are circular areas that curve from a flat floor to a vertical wall at least two or three times the combatants' heights.

Under low-gravity conditions, muscle-powered flight becomes a common activity to those seeking new thrills. It is only possible to fly near the sunline of a Vivarium cylinder, or the center of an O'Neill-type cylinder. Gliding at lower altitudes is possible, but safety regulations do not permit flight below two hundred meters above mean ground level. The domes on the Moon are not large or high enough for safety, but people can soar at lower elevations on Mars where the atmosphere is thickest. Most flight apparatis are constructed from lightweight composites and polymers, and have a compact safety chute in case the user loses control or lift.

▼ EXO-BALL

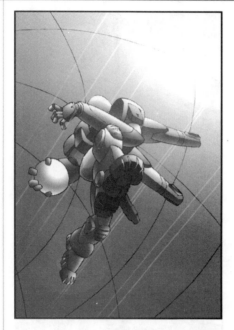

Exo-ball has begun to catch on among other space colonies with patrons willing to support the formation of a team and pay for the construction of the facilities. As in the Jovian teams, the most successful exo-ball teams have members with ESWAT and military backgrounds. Most non-Jovian exo-ball teams are part of the newly formed leagues that have set out their rules explicitly from the beginning; thus, they have avoided some of the rules conflicts experienced by the wide range of Jovian rules variations prior to the formation of the formal Jovian exo-ball league. As yet, there have been no formal matches between teams from different nations, partly because of different rules sets and partly because of the political situation in the Solar System. Undoubtedly there will be some intense national rivalries formed when international exo-ball competitions are finally held.

Exo-ball is played between four to eight players wearing heavily modified exo-suits. The game is played with a highly elastic ball that the players must pass to each member of the team before they throw the ball into the common goal at the "bottom" of the spherical arena. Physical contact between players is strictly forbidden. This rule produces some truly astounding displays of piloting skill as players twist and turn to avoid hitting each other.

▼ CLIMBING

The partial terraforming of Mars makes it a climber's paradise. Wearing light Mars suits, the Valles Marinaris and the interiors of the various large craters and canyons are regular climbing spots. Recreational and sport climbing are popular activities on Mars, and a large part of the tourist industry that caters to people wishing to experience the Martian environment involves climbing tours. Climbing hostels and shops are located at the base and summit of the most popular climbing locations. Equipment rentals cost between 50 to 150 credits per day depending on the type and quantities of equipment needed. Extended climbing excursions, such as the interior of Olympus Mons, require hiring a guide for an average of 250 credits per day if the climbers are inexperienced or are unfamiliar with the climb route.

Some very adventurous people climb in an environment with no atmosphere: Earth's Moon, outer planet moons and asteroids. The equipment they use — spacesuits with climbing gear — is specially designed for the location's conditions. The training and preparations for these difficult challenges are closely akin to early expeditions to conquer Mount Everest on Earth.

▼ MARS BIATHLON

While the biathlon of Earth involves skiing and shooting, the Mars biathlon involves distance running and climbing. All biathlons involve climbing down one side of a Mars canyon, a run across the length or width of the canyon, and finishing with the climb up the opposite canyon wall. Some events encompass several smaller canyons or craters, while some events cover the greatest features of Mars. The greatest of these events is Trans-Valles Marineris Biathlon, followed by the Olympus Mons Challenge. There is a starting line, a finish line, and numerous checkpoints in between that competitors must reach within a specific time frame, or be disqualified. The route between checkpoints is left entirely to the competitors.

Since the longer events require many days and nights on the Martian surface, the competitors cache supplies along their intended route. These caches are either placed in secret prior to the event, or placed by race officials at competitor-specified points in sealed and code-locked containers provided by the competitors. It is against competition regulations to break into, destroy, hide or relocate official supply containers, and will result in the competitor being disqualified from the race and banned from competition for five Mars years, or ten Earth years. It is not unknown for competitors to borrow a few supplies from a fellow competitor's secret caches, if they can find them. Most competitors will only do so if they are very low on supplies and have a significant distance to go before reaching their own supplies. If competitors are out of supplies or injured, they are expected to activate their emergency locator beacon for immediate pickup.

SPACE RACING ▼

There are any number of locations throughout the Solar System where people race space vehicles of all kinds: fighters, exo-suits, exo-armors, full-sized vessels or anything spaceworthy people are willing to bet on. Many of the competitions are informal events that are organized on short notice. The most common of these events are MMU and M-pod races between the many space construction crews. The friendly rivalry between crews and shifts is tolerated by employers if the project is on schedule, no equipment is damaged and no one is hurt. Some companies even hold formal competitions for their employees and with other companies. The races are often conducted as duels over insults or slights between crews.

Exo-suit racing is another popular sport. These races require an exo-suit pilot to navigate an obstacle course under partial or zero gravity conditions. Some stations and colony cylinders have built contained tracks inside, outside and through their structures for the purposes of exo-suit racing. Actually building these tracks requires a large investment, but the resulting profits can quickly recover the costs. Both exo-ball and exo-suit racing are rapidly growing in popularity for their displays of skill and challenges to the competitors. Surplus space fighters and exo-armors are also used for racing, though usually through a larger course that can take them through several orbits of a planet or moon. Some have even been outfitted with practice weapons and scoring sensors for broadcasts of mock wargames. These matches are always popular, and are often undertaken by ex-military pilots looking for thrills without the danger.

SOLAR SAILING ▼

Humanity sailed the seas and oceans of Earth for many centuries for exploration, trade and sport. In the 23rd century, sailing through space has replaced sailing through the polluted waters of Earth. With faster means of travel available, solar sailing remains a challenging sport to master, and is exclusively the domain of the Mercurian Merchant Guild for commercial purposes. As such, the most successful solar sail racers are ex-Merchant Guild sail barge crew members. Some of the more successful non-Guild racers have put in time on a Guild solar sail ship as working passengers. The winner in solar sail races is determined by a complex system of calculations based on craft weight, sail area (itself governed by racing classes) and time to complete the route. The Solar Cup Race is a quintennial (every five years) solar sailing race from Mercury to Venus. Most of the entries are custom-built sailcraft or commercial designs modified for smaller crews and speed. The race has strict rules for maximum sail diameter, required components and mass.

TYPICAL SOLAR RACER ▥

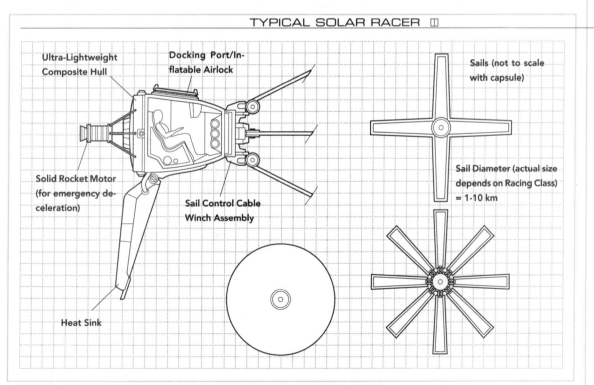

Ultra-Lightweight Composite Hull

Docking Port/Inflatable Airlock

Sails (not to scale with capsule)

Solid Rocket Motor (for emergency deceleration)

Sail Control Cable Winch Assembly

Sail Diameter (actual size depends on Racing Class) = 1-10 km

Heat Sink

▶ ENTERTAINMENT

For some, entertainment could be described as any activity that occurs outside of normal occupational activities; indeed, many people do classify entertainment as anything other than their "usual" job. Many of the people that live beyond Earth's atmosphere are raised with a certain ethic that precludes any long periods of idleness, so that after they finish their regular duties they will still be doing something.

Passive or active participation in some form of entertainment is always part of a person's daily activities, with many people choosing to be actively involved in some sort of artistic endeavor during their week. While sports activities have their appeal and benefits, entertainment pursuits generally cost less to participate in, and are more inclusive to a wider range of people.

▼ VIDEO & TRIDEO

Local video and trideo program providers, as well as SysInstruum sources, offer a wide variety of video and trideo to the public. Sports, historical dramas, soap operas, space operas, computer-generated animation, comedy, news, talk shows, political and military commentary, finances and reruns of early programs are all available. All of these programs and any number of newly developed shows are available to audiences across the Solar System. Historical dramas based on the early days of space exploration are the most popular programs in the Solar System. There are also any number of amateur productions transmitted as part of public service channels, while there are even more amateur productions available as short segments from the SysInstruum. Local programs, and selected Solar System-wide programs, are included with the cost of renting quarters.

▼ VIRTUAL REALITY

The possibilities of virtual reality technologies have led to the quick adoption of a wide variety of hardware suited to the needs and affluence of varying demographic groups. Limited virtual reality is the most common mode of experiencing VR, with immersive VR a distant second. The barrier for immersion technology is the vast expense of the feedback suit, which has proven prohibitive to all but the most dedicated VR fanatics. Much more common than the immersion suit is a simple set of trackers placed at key points on the body; these allow the user to move normally in the virtual environment, albeit without any tactile feedback. Besides their use for experiencing the innumerable fantasies generated by the human mind, virtual reality technology is widely used for education and training. Most VR sets have enough interactivity to be used for mechanical telepresence over a short range.

▼ LITERATURE

The number of written works available to the public is staggering. All publicly available works are freely available for download from the SysInstruum, with hundreds to thousands of new works being added daily. Because of the deluge of new material, it is hard for an author to gain a wide audience without the support of a public relations campaign to raise awareness about the author's work. That support is usually not forthcoming unless the author has produced something that truly sets their work above the rest. Few people in the last century have come close to the national popularity of a writer like that obtained by the Confederation's Elisabeth Bisset, let alone that level of popularity across entire Solar System.

Not all written material is guaranteed for its accuracy or veracity, no matter what the author claims. Scholarly journals and printed news sources require payment of a fee for access, but the material is certified to be accurate and truthful by the profession's regulating body. People making false claims leading to personal injury or distress are treated severely under the law of most nations. In an environment where trust and accurate information can mean the difference between life and death, anything that jeopardizes peoples' well-being is simply not tolerated.

MUSIC ▼

Live music performances are extremely popular throughout the Solar System, and not just for the music alone. Performances often incorporate visual elements from simple video to full holographic presentations to accompany the music. The most popular music styles include full orchestral and electronic pieces that cover the classics to a wide range of styles for small bands. Many people enjoy playing a musical instrument, and are often part of amateur musical groups if they regularly perform music, privately or publicly. The close proximity of everything within an artificial environment means that loud noises can be heard by many neighbors, so heavy bass is considered extremely rude and barbaric. That is not to say percussion does not have its place, but it is used sparingly. All colony cylinders have at least one outdoor amphitheater for music and theatrical productions. The acoustics of these facilities are spectacular, with the occasional, minimal augmentation of voices and instruments by the sound system. Most of these facilities are open to the air, so directional speakers that broadcast "black" noise surround the amphitheater perimeter to contain the sound, with smaller black noise systems available for personal use to contain sound locally. For extremely popular presentations, it is normal practice to shut off the containment speakers and charge a minimal fee for standing-room-only admission for several blocks surrounding the amphitheater.

Electronic works use the sophisticated and widely available sound editing and recording software that is available for purchase and for free (though the former is always more versatile and has better sound quality.) Using built-in and custom-recorded sound samples, each sound or note can be modified to fit the composer's requirements exactly. While Edicts restrictions limit the development of artificial intelligence, this has not stopped some from trying to generate computer programs that write original works for performance. Most performances of music generated solely by these programs have been met with ambivalence and poor reviews. Performances that have excelled are overshadowed by suspicions that a composer modifies the music to improve the quality of the piece.

HOLST'S THE PLANETS ★

One of the symphonic favorites of the past decade are holographically enhanced performances of Gustav Holst's *The Planets*. The original symphonic suite consisted of seven movements, with each movement named for a known planet at the time it was written between 1914 and 1916: Mars, the Bringer of War; Venus, the Bringer of Peace; Mercury, the Winged Messenger; Jupiter, the Bringer of Jollity; Saturn, the Bringer of Old Age; Uranus, the Magician; and Neptune, the Mystic. The suite's paper score was carried with Venusian immigrants, and survived the Fall (unlike many other pieces whose digital recordings perished during the Long Winter). During the late 23rd century, composer and holographic artist Johan Wiser added an eighth movement, Earth, the Bringer of Life, as a tribute to the seeming reunion of all the colonies with the mother planet. The eighth movement uses many modern instruments and, while not universally accepted, is generally seen as the first sign of the new era of artistic endeavor.

5.2.4

5.2.5

HISTORICAL FACTS

FINE ARTS ▼

The effects of a monochrome environment on humans are well documented. This results in a wide range of commissioned (and uncommissioned) artworks for the open spaces and walls of the any habitat. The owners of some buildings will often allow an artist to paint the interior or exterior based on a theme. Painted artwork is generally limited to civilian vessels, and often to the discretion of the crew members within limits set by the captain. The hull is often finished with a variety of colors and shades that are cycled to improve morale and pride in their vessel. Within the vessel, various walls are painted in different colors and mosaics to help crews living in confined spaces. Military vessels usually have an unofficial ship's logo painted on the hull, while the wall panels are rotated between differently-colored panels.

Live drama productions enjoy wide popularity. From simple, single-person street performances to fully staged productions at local theater venues, the body of work to perform from is immense and varied, and grows each day; many more works of classical text survived the Fall than did music. Many vessels with larger crews have a theater group that practices and performs at each port they stop in, or for the rest of the crew along the way.

The limited space of an artificial environment leads to smaller sculpted pieces, or holographic projections that are easily stored in computer memory. Most galleries and museums try to maximize the presentation space available, but there are still limits. Painting and computer-generated image construction are both common visual-art pursuits. CGI artwork has the additional properties of being compact and animated at the same time, two attributes that make it highly attractive to space-conscious practitioners.

GAME RESOURCES

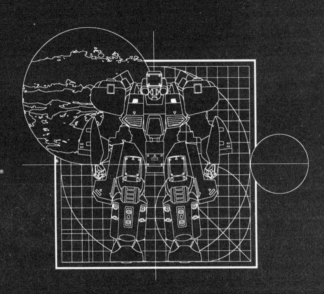

The great enemy of clear language is insincerity.
— George Orwell

A BRIEF GUIDE TO SPACER'S RUNIC ◄

Spacer's Runic is a written language — using ideograms — created by spacers during the late 21st century as an alternate or emergency form of communication when speaking wasn't possible. The straight lines and dots used for the words of the Spacer's Runic lexicon facilitate the use of improvised tools and surfaces for writing messages almost anywhere. As a matter of practicality, people who perform EVA tasks regularly carry both temporary and permanent markers for writing messages in Spacer's Runic. The array of ideograms has grown very large during the past century, so only a small portion of the lexicon is provided here.

Combined with the use of Morse Code, Spacer's Runic is the only truly universal language, though it did develop some different dialects as the result of isolation after the Fall. Morse Code is considered to be part of the Spacer's Runic lexicon by many, so anyone with at least one level in Spacer's Runic (and a working knowledge of a Latin-based language) also knows Morse Code. It is easy to use, and often used when communications fail, through the blinking of running lights on a vessel or any other light source.

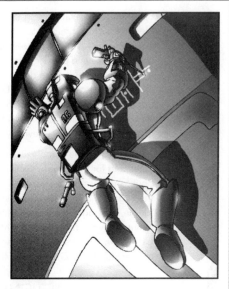

GRAMMAR AND SYNTAX ▼

Grammar in Spacer's Runic is kept to an absolute minimum, with only a few syntactic marks and spacing conventions serving to help clarify intent or meaning. Spacer's Runic is read from left to right, top to bottom. A single straight line is used to indicate the left side, and orientation, of the ideograms as written. Given that orientation is relative in microgravity, this convention is the most important to ensuring timely translation. The orientation mark must include at least two lines of ideograms to ensure clarity, though it is common to extend the mark to encompass all lines. A message that is only a single line will have the mark extend above and below the line of ideograms.

An ideogram consists of a set of dots and straight lines drawn within a 3 x 3 grid of evenly sized squares. Dots are drawn in the center of a square or at the intersections of the grid; lines are drawn from one side of a square to another, either from an intersection or the midpoint. The author does not strictly need to follow this structure, but it must be reasonably consistent to avoid confusion. It is understood that the ideograms are likely written under stress, but clarity on the part of the author is still required to communicate effectively, especially if warning of danger.

Each line of ideograms starts at the orientation mark with new ideograms being added to the right of the last ideogram. Each line is thought of as a single sentence, but there is a symbol that marks the continuation of the sentence on the next line. The convention for spacing each ideogram requires the width of one ideogram between each ideogram, but no more space than two full ideograms in width. One exception to this rule allows each digit in a number to be placed closely together.

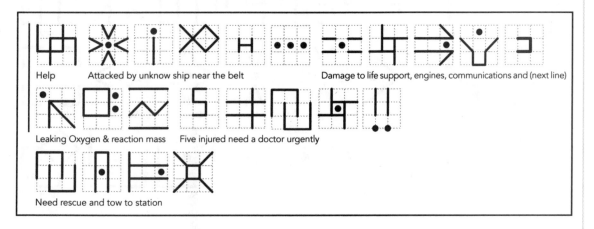

Help   Attacked by unknow ship near the belt   Damage to life support, engines, communications and (next line)

Leaking Oxygen & reaction mass   Five injured need a doctor urgently

Need rescue and tow to station

GAME RESOURCES

▼ USING SPACER'S RUNIC IN THE GAME

Basic space survival training (Space Survival Level 1 or greater) includes all the necessary Spacer's Runic ideograms to communicate basic emergency information. Personnel are able to describe the situation in general terms, and can request supplies and assistance. Level 1 skill allows a character to conduct simple conversations and provide information beyond the requirements of an emergency situation. A person with this skill level could make do travelling anywhere in the Solar System. Messages that are technical in nature require the users have at least Level 2 language proficiency. While Players and Gamemasters are not expected to learn Spacer's Runic themselves, the following pages contain a wide range of useful ideograms. And since this brief dictionary is far from complete, Players and Gamemasters are encouraged to add new ideograms of their own devisory.

Depending on the complexity of the content, and the length, of the message, the Gamemaster assigns a Threshold for a Language Skill Test. Subtract the Margin of Success from, or add the Margin of Failure to, double the assigned Threshold to determine the number of minutes the message takes to write out. A message will always take at least one minute to write. For example, Sara's character is writing a long, yet simple, message with an assigned Threshold of 3. She rolls an MoS of 1, so it takes her character five minutes to write the message. The suitability of a given tool for writing may add or subtract from the Threshold. To read the resulting message, the reader must roll a Language Skill Test against the same Threshold, subtracting the MoS, or adding the MoF.

▥ DICTIONARY OF IDEOGRAMS

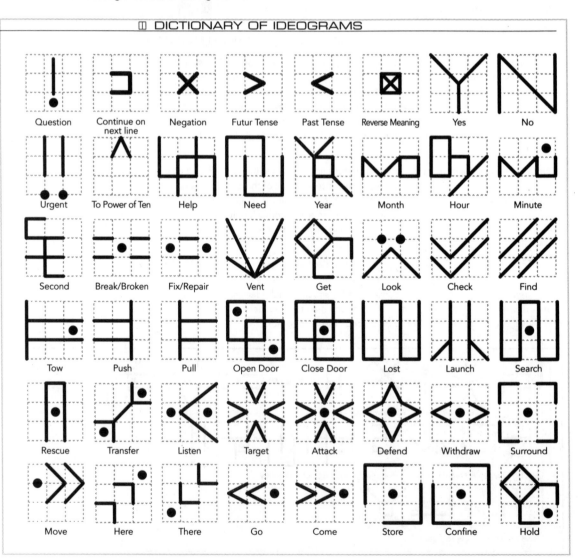

Question	Continue on next line	Negation	Futur Tense	Past Tense	Reverse Meaning	Yes	No
Urgent	To Power of Ten	Help	Need	Year	Month	Hour	Minute
Second	Break/Broken	Fix/Repair	Vent	Get	Look	Check	Find
Tow	Push	Pull	Open Door	Close Door	Lost	Launch	Search
Rescue	Transfer	Listen	Target	Attack	Defend	Withdraw	Surround
Move	Here	There	Go	Come	Store	Confine	Hold

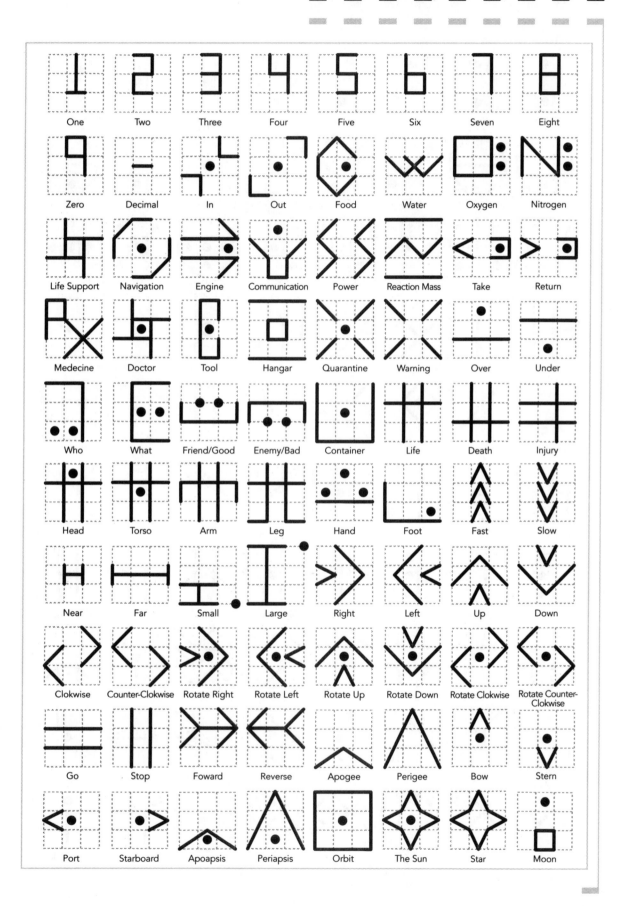

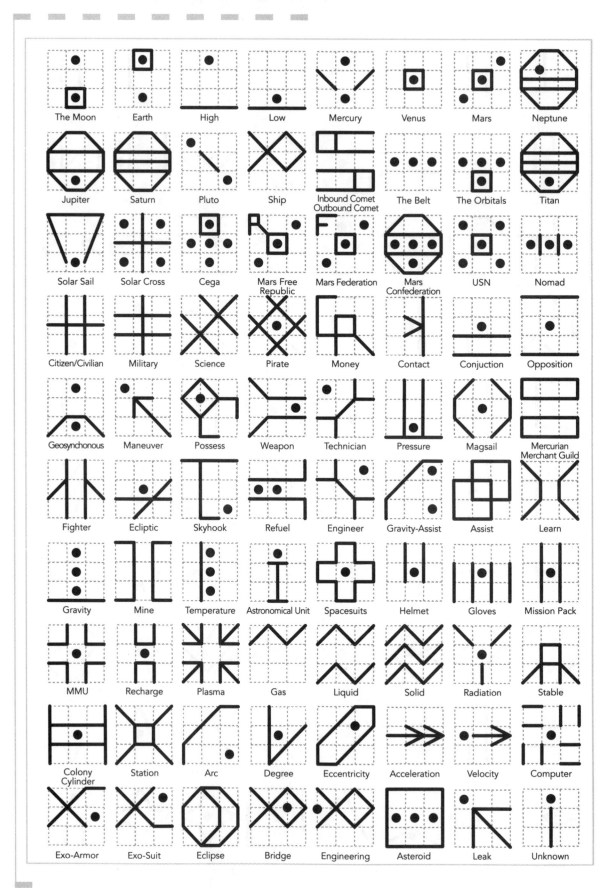

The Moon | Earth | High | Low | Mercury | Venus | Mars | Neptune

Jupiter | Saturn | Pluto | Ship | Inbound Comet / Outbound Comet | The Belt | The Orbitals | Titan

Solar Sail | Solar Cross | Cega | Mars Free Republic | Mars Federation | Mars Confederation | USN | Nomad

Citizen/Civilian | Military | Science | Pirate | Money | Contact | Conjuction | Opposition

Geosynchonous | Maneuver | Possess | Weapon | Technician | Pressure | Magsail | Mercurian Merchant Guild

Fighter | Ecliptic | Skyhook | Refuel | Engineer | Gravity-Assist | Assist | Learn

Gravity | Mine | Temperature | Astronomical Unit | Spacesuits | Helmet | Gloves | Mission Pack

MMU | Recharge | Plasma | Gas | Liquid | Solid | Radiation | Stable

Colony Cylinder | Station | Arc | Degree | Eccentricity | Acceleration | Velocity | Computer

Exo-Armor | Exo-Suit | Eclipse | Bridge | Engineering | Asteroid | Leak | Unknown

SEARCH AND RESCUE TECHNICIAN ▼

Outside of being a combat pilot, being a search and rescue technician is one of the most dangerous jobs in the Solar System. Walking into an unknown and potentially dangerous situation is just one of the occupational hazards that goes with the job. While most of the time the work is fairly ordinary, search and rescue technicians are some of the most highly trained and professional people in the Solar System when the situation is at its worst; one need only talk to those saved by these extraordinary people.

Part medic and part mechanic, the search and rescue technician is the first person to come to the aid of people on a vessel in distress. Besides their training in emergency medicine, they are trained in damage control procedures, since they may be called to stabilize the situation to get to victims safely. Search and rescue technicians are trained to never enter an area until it is stable; an unsafe rescue is all too likely to become a situation in which both the victim and the SAR technicians need help.

Search and rescue technicians are serious and methodical people that are dedicated to saving lives. Many are driven by personal experience with disaster, or have been traumatized by the disasters they have witnessed. They are all too familiar with the dangers of space, and are ever-vigilant in seeking to protect those that have the misfortune of being a victim.

ATTRIBUTES ◇

AGI	+1	APP	0	BUI	0	CRE	0	FIT	0
INF	0	KNO	+1	PER	0	PSY	0	WIL	+1
STR	0	HEA	0	STA	25	UD	3	AD	3

SKILLS ◇

Skill	Level	Attr.	Skill	Level	Attr.	Skill	Level	Attr.	Skill	Level	Attr.
Computers	1	+1	Exo Pilot	1	+1	Mechanics	2	+1	Space Survival	2	0
Electronics	1	+1	First Aid	3	+1	Notice	2	0	Zero-G Movement	2	+1

EQUIPMENT AND COST ◇

Typical Equipment:	SAR tools, hard spacesuit
Salary:	40,000 to 60,000 credits/year
Basic Costs:	19 Character Points, 30 Skill Points

ACTION CAMPAIGN USES ◇

Action means physical damage of both people and machines, though the search and rescue technician is better equipped to deal with the former. Not only can they patch people up, but they can help patch up most anything else. This makes them useful in any number of situations, and not just for the aftermath, either.

INTRIGUE CAMPAIGN USES ◇

When a covert operation goes wrong, the search and rescue vessels arrives to help, oblivious to the web of intrigue that they are about to be stuck in. Perhaps the people rescued were working on Edicts-violating technology, contaminating the rescue vessel, or, with her dying breath, a rescued spy slips an SAR tech the design documents for a prototype exo-amor, warship, or weapon.

POSSIBLE VARIATIONS ◇

Search and rescue technicians are employed by both civilian, military and paramilitary organizations in a number of roles. Search and rescue technician in the military will have basic combat training, not to mention access to additional equipment that is not normally widely available to civilians. Being highly trained already, some personnel opt for more combat training to become combat medics for special forces units.

POSSIBLE SUBPLOTS ◇

Nothing frustrates a search and rescue technician more than not being able to help someone in distress. They hate it even more if the reason for their inaction is politically motivated. A badly damaged commercial ship is discovered drifting out of the asteroid belt by the rescue ship. The search and rescue technicians start their work of stabilizing the situation and evacuating casualties when a warship arrives, demanding that the rescue crew turn over all personnel from the ship.

GAME RESOURCES

▼ GHOST

Whatever the reason for a person becoming a Ghost, they have accepted their new life without reservation or regret. For some reason, the Ghost became disenchanted with life as most other people live. By nature, Ghosts are always solitary and shy. It is not difficult to hide oneself among the machinery, nor is difficult to find what is needed. Most people who become Ghosts are technically proficient, or become proficient. Part of their life involves "borrowing" what they need, and what they need comes from the systems that support the colony cylinder.

Most Ghosts prefer to remain invisible. The only indications of their existence in a locale are the mysterious repairs, modifications or changes made to systems in the area a Ghost "haunts." Ghosts often move between several locations to prevent someone from noticing their borrowing. The locations they choose as their "home" will have everything they need within a reasonable distance, and have several access and egress. Hidden stashes of supplies and useful items are kept in other locations so that the Ghost is not affected by the discovery of his primary living area. Many Ghosts do have some contact with a few selected people they trust or have received help from. In fact, those that discover a Ghost but act as though they saw nothing are likelier than most to earn his gratitude and cautious friendship.

◇ ATTRIBUTES

AGI	0	APP	-1	BUI	0	CRE	+1	FIT	0
INF	0	KNO	+1	PER	+1	PSY	0	WIL	0
STR	0	HEA	0	STA	25	UD	3	AD	3

◇ SKILLS

Skill	Level	Attr.	Skill	Level	Attr.	Skill	Level	Attr.	Skill	Level	Attr.
Computers	1	+1	Mechanics	1	+1	Stealth	1	0	Survival (Space)	1	+1
Electronics	2	+1	Notice	2	+1	Streetwise	2	0	Tinker	2	+1

◇ EQUIPMENT AND COST

Typical Equipment:	Worn-out coveralls, simple tools
Salary:	None
Basic Costs:	18 Character Points, 28 Skill Points

◇ ACTION CAMPAIGN USES

Ghosts avoid conflict entirely; they are not equipped to deal with violence, nor do they care about the conflicts of others (they would not be a Ghost if they did). That being said, someone who views the Ghost as a threat could make the Ghost the object of a manhunt. This will lead to all sorts of interesting adventures as the Ghost attempts to stay ahead of the hunters, and, quite possibly, fight back with traps to discourage pursuit.

◇ INTRIGUE CAMPAIGN USES

Who better to see what happens in the shadows than a Ghost? A Ghost will have access to all kinds of interesting places on a colony cylinder, or the means to get to places otherwise unvisited or unnoticed. As a means of support, Ghosts sometimes cultivate discreet contacts among the cylinder's population that can provide reciprocal favors for something the Ghost can provide. Most times this contact is by anonymous means, and always in exchange for useful tools and supplies.

◇ POSSIBLE VARIATIONS

Playing a Ghost against the stereotype is an interesting idea given the general assumptions people make about these whispers of rumor. People that choose this course for themselves have motives other than escape. For example, it is an excellent means to conduct certain businesses with anonymity and freedom of movement. True Ghosts will likely seek to interfere with such activities, however. Reorganizing some of the skills easily creates a high-tech cat burglar.

◇ POSSIBLE SUBPLOTS

One of the Player Characters is contacted by an old friend who now lives his life as a Ghost. He says has important information, and it relates to something the PCs are currently involved with. The only problem now is finding him. Instead of the Ghost they were expecting to meet, someone else is found nosing around the meet area.

SPACE TRAFFIC CONTROLLER ▼

Space traffic controllers watch over the expert system computers that monitor and direct the actual traffic in the control zones. Often former navigators or pilots, these people are familiar with both sides of the dance of space traffic. Many of the people who have become space traffic controllers were bored by the lack of work for them between departure and arrival. Most also have training in other areas like communications and sensor systems. This training also provides them with excellent qualifications to become a space traffic controller, and now they are always busy.

Even the most automated STC systems require human oversight to prevent mistakes. The typical work day of a space traffic controller is filled with system checks, flight plan verifications, traffic handoffs as vessels move between zones, requests to change or modify orbits, vessels that declare emergencies, vessels moving to their final destinations, transitions between the STC zone and local control zones and any number of procedural, computational or administrative tasks that need attention. Smaller, less traveled zones are usually fairly quiet, but the major zones around the planets are always busy. Many controllers will take a leave of absence from this hectic pace to serve a tour aboard a commercial vessel before returning to space traffic control. These personnel are highly sought after for their intimate knowledge of the STC systems, and are often the most efficient means of navigating the control zones.

ATTRIBUTES ◇

AGI	0	APP	0	BUI	0	CRE	+1	FIT	0
INF	0	KNO	+2	PER	0	PSY	0	WIL	0
STR	0	HEA	0	STA	25	UD	3	AD	3

SKILLS ◇

Skill	Level	Attr.	Skill	Level	Attr.	Skill	Level	Attr.	Skill	Level	Attr.
Communications	1	+2	Elec. Warfare	2	+2	Space Navigation	2	+2	Space Survival	1	+1
Computer	2	+2	Physical Sciences	1	+2	Space Pilot	1	+1	Zero-G Movement	1	0

EQUIPMENT AND COST ◇

Typical Equipment:	Portable computer, PDA (navigation regulations)
Salary:	50,000 to 75,000 credits/year
Basic Costs:	21 Character Points, 32 Skill Points

ACTION CAMPAIGN USES ◇

The extensive sensor system used to monitor space traffic is very useful for avoiding hunters or following prey. A controller is an invaluable ally for seeing through the chaos of battle, tracking everything within range of his STC sensors. When involved in combat, it is all too easy to lose track of what is happening; a controller can help a pilot keep his bearings — and perhaps his life.

INTRIGUE CAMPAIGN USES ◇

"I was never here, and no auxiliary craft departed from that ship." When people want to hide their comings and goings they must deal with the people who keep track of the traffic in the STC zones. Space traffic controllers taking bribes to turn a blind eye to certain traffic is a disturbingly common occurrence. Short of being an STC system technician, space traffic controllers are intimately familiar with the STC systems and the peculiarities of their control zones.

POSSIBLE VARIATIONS ◇

In the wet navies on Earth, they are called the air combat controllers, but in space they are referred to as flight operations officers. They are responsible for the launch and recovery of all auxiliary craft, from M-pods to exo-armors. This is no easy job, especially when trying to recover a battle-damaged craft low on reaction mass and missing half its control thrusters. They are also responsible for directing fighters and exo-armors during combat.

POSSIBLE SUBPLOTS ◇

The tabloids are rife with stories of top secret warships and exo-armors. Something strange is occurring at the edge of the STC sensor areas, so the on-duty controller duly notes the occurrences. The next day, tabloid reporters are swarming the controller asking about the secret goings of aliens and military projects. What to do about this sudden attention?

GAME RESOURCES

▼ CUSTOMS OFFICER

To most people, customs officers are just another kind of law enforcement. They are much more than that, however, since they deal with a wide range of often complicated and dense laws, and the bureaucracy that accompanies those laws. They deal with people on a regular basis and are always watchful for the subtle signals that things are not as they seem. Through all the changes that have occurred since the establishment of humans in space, nations still jealously guard their borders in whatever form. This means ensuring that what enters and leaves the nation is considered safe and in the nation's best interest. From people to products, anything that crosses a nation's border is subject to the approval of a customs officer.

Customs officers are always busy performing inspections and talking to arriving travelers. The most visible presence of the customs officer is that encountered by people entering and leaving the nation. All commercial passengers and crews must pass through a customs office whenever they wish to move beyond the vessel's confines. Behind the scenes, customs officers are inspecting cargo against manifests and collecting duties on products. On occasion they also board vessels to search for known or suspected infractions against the laws and regulations of the nation. Of course, there is also all the paperwork to do that goes with being part of a government department.

◇ ATTRIBUTES

AGI	+1	APP	0	BUI	0	CRE	0	FIT	0
INF	0	KNO	+1	PER	+1	PSY	0	WIL	0
STR	0	HEA	0	STA	25	UD	3	AD	3

◇ SKILLS

Skill	Level	Attr.	Skill	Level	Attr.	Skill	Level	Attr.	Skill	Level	Attr.
Bureaucracy	2	+1	Human Perception	1	0	Law *	1	+1	Small Arms	2	+1
Dodge	1	+1	Investigation	1	+1	Notice	2	+1	Zero-G Movement	1	+1
* (Customs & Immigration)											

◇ EQUIPMENT AND COST

Typical Equipment:	Uniform, sidearm, PDA (regulations, schedules, duties), contraband scanner
Salary:	30,000 to 50,000 credits/year
Basic Costs:	19 Character Points, 29 Skill Points

◇ ACTION CAMPAIGN USES

As law enforcement officers who specialize in customs and immigration matters, customs officers are in conflict with smugglers, fugitives and anyone else trying to break the laws they enforce. Boarding and searching vessels is a common occurrence, and one that occasionally escalates when the offender believes a fight is preferable to the alternatives.

◇ INTRIGUE CAMPAIGN USES

With their knowledge of customs procedures, officers know all the holes in the system for sneaking just about anything onto a station or into a habitat. Whether it is contraband for the black market, or spies for an enemy nation, they are the men and women responsible for overseeing the flow of goods and people into a nation. Whether they interfere with or aid the intrigues that occur at the border, a customs officer is always just around the corner.

◇ POSSIBLE VARIATIONS

A customs official is placed behind a desk to handle all the paperwork that accompanies the people and goods that enter into a nation each day. As such, their primary vocational Skills include Computers and Investigation instead of the combat Skills required to deal with people attempting to circumvent customs regulations and laws.

◇ POSSIBLE SUBPLOTS

An internal investigation of the customs officer, whether the allegations are true or not, can place profound stresses on relationships and job performance. Such pressure can, at times, even cause previously honest officers to go bad. Also, unwittingly exposing a friendly undercover agent during the performance of their duties has all sorts of consequences for officer, the agent, and the investigation being undertaken at the time.

CARGO MASTER ▼

The cargo master knows his cargo docks better than any other person. He can tell a person virtually anything about the cargo on the docks: schedules for arriving and departing shipments, the contents of cargo containers, and the rumors an arriving crew brings. Cargo masters are some of the most accomplished businesspeople in the Solar System. The transactions they perform on a daily basis can account for millions of credits of goods and resources. The busiest cargo docks will have numerous vessels moving cargo to and fro at any given moment. It is the cargo master's responsibility to coordinate all this activity.

Cargo masters are in regular contact with customs and government officials. Since it is normal practice to sell or purchase contracts from the people doing business with the cargo dock, the cargo master must ensure that regulations are followed, and that any duties, tariffs or fees are paid. Accompanying customs inspectors is another duty that cargo masters are sometimes involved with.

Finally, the constant and regular contact with commercial crews from across the Solar System means that the cargo master is fount of obscure and valuable information. The cargo master often uses this intimate knowledge of unofficial goings-on in the Solar System to cut a better deal, or even to avoid a deal altogether. Since all these rumors and stories are not always true, it is the sign of a truly successful cargo master to discern what is useful.

ATTRIBUTES ◇

AGI	0	APP	0	BUI	0	CRE	0	FIT	0
INF	+1	KNO	+1	PER	+1	PSY	0	WIL	0
STR	0	HEA	0	STA	25	UD	3	AD	3

SKILLS ◇

Skill	Level	Attr.	Skill	Level	Attr.	Skill	Level	Attr.	Skill	Level	Attr.
Business	2	+1	Exo-Pilot	1	0	Notice	2	+1	Zero-G Movement	2	0
Computer	1	+1	Haggling	2	+1	Space Survival	1	0	Streetwise	1	+1

EQUIPMENT AND COST ◇

Typical Equipment:	PDA (cargo yard records)
Salary:	40,000 to 65,000 credits/year, up to 500,000 credits/year if involved in illegal activities
Basic Costs:	19 Character Points, 28 Skill Points

ACTION CAMPAIGN USES ◇

A cargo master can serve in the military as a quartermaster or supply technician. While they don't have any combat experience themselves, they are likely to know who to call if some muscle is required. Cargo yards are also strategic resources, so they are likely to be subject to attack, and are defended accordingly.

INTRIGUE CAMPAIGN USES ◇

The cargo master knows every container that enters or leaves his yard, so when containers start disappearing, it is the cargo master that notices. Even more interesting is that the missing containers all contain very mundane items, according to the manifests. Are some of the yard workers trying to make a buck on the side, or is there something else in those containers?

POSSIBLE VARIATIONS ◇

Many cargo masters have served as quartermasters in the military. This military service will make them even more hard-nosed about their dealings. This also means they will have contacts within the military establishment that can provide valuable information not normally available to civilians. Of course, those friends in the military receive due compensation from the cargo master for such information.

POSSIBLE SUBPLOTS ◇

The cargo master is approached by "persons of questionable reputation" to allow the use of the cargo yard as a channel for illegal shipments, with or without willing cooperation. The choices, and the consequences, of acceptance and subsequent actions provide a multitude of opportunities for adventure.

GAME RESOURCES

▼ PASSENGER STEWARD

Stewards aboard commercial vessels are tasked with the difficult job of keeping the passengers happy during the often long trips between the planets. While crews are kept busy by virtue of their duties, passenger boredom can cause problems for the crew. Most passenger stewards specialize in one or two activities that are regularly scheduled for passengers. From painting classes to elegant formal dinner parties, activities for every passenger are offered at some point.

When a passenger vessel arrives at its destination, it is time for the stewards to relax and unwind before the vessel departs for its next destination. Exploring the local sights is not only something a steward can enjoy, but is also considered occupational training as they can better inform passengers of the most interesting places to visit. If stewards are expected to be on-site for an extended period, they will often assist the local travel company staff in the office. Stewards also have the option of taking some time away from shipboard duties by taking an office position, thus giving another staff member the chance to travel.

◇ ATTRIBUTES

AGI	0	APP	+1	BUI	-1	CRE	+1	FIT	0
INF	+1	KNO	0	PER	0	PSY	+1	WIL	0
STR	0	HEA	0	STA	25	UD	3	AD	3

◇ SKILLS

Skill	Level	Attr.	Skill	Level	Attr.	Skill	Level	Attr.	Skill	Level	Attr.
Business	1	0	Human Perception	2	+1	Music	*	+1	Visual Art	*	+1
Cooking	*	+1	Literature	*	+1	Space Survival	2	+1	Zero-G Movement	1	0
Etiquette	2	0									

* Choose three of these four skills with two at Level 2 and one at Level 1.

◇ EQUIPMENT AND COST

Typical Equipment:	PDA (passenger information, activity schedules, recipes, book lists, music lists, etc.)
Salary:	25,000 to 50,000 credits/year plus bonuses
Basic Costs:	19 Character Points, 28 Skill Points

◇ ACTION CAMPAIGN USES

Stewards with combat training often serve as security personnel for passenger vessels. Some stewards come from military service backgrounds that grant them limited combat skills, but many also have training in first aid and damage control procedures. These people are highly sought after by civilian passenger lines for their ability to assist passengers and crew during emergencies.

◇ INTRIGUE CAMPAIGN USES

The frequent travel of stewards makes them the ideal carriers (cooperative or not) for information and other discreet items. Being a steward is also an ideal cover for professional intelligence agents to travel anonymously. Agents using this cover often have access to passenger quarters, so it is entirely possible to dig for information within the quarters of any VIPs onboard.

◇ POSSIBLE VARIATIONS

As mentioned above, stewards with combat training can act as bodyguards to VIPs while acting as personal staff. The stewards are highly paid for their services, their discretion and ,often, their silence. All such bodyguards are proficient in both small arms and unarmed, or melee, combat. There is plenty of flexibility and cross-training in areas of activity undertaken other by Player Characters to help keep morale high while actively contributing to the team's mission.

◇ POSSIBLE SUBPLOTS

Friction between rivals in a cruise becomes heated, and places a steward in middle. Even though it is his job to keep the passengers happy, this intervention earns him the enmity of one or both parties. Whatever the outcome, the former passenger will do everything in his power to make the steward's life miserable as repayment for the slight.

MARTIAN BIATHLETE ▼

Martian biathlons are considered the ultimate in competitive sports. The challenges to a biathlete's psychological and physical toughness and skills are monumental. Combined with immense size of the Martian terrain and still-deadly atmosphere, Martian biathletes are held as equals to the challenges they face; they are among the few people widely known and respected across the divided planet. Almost all biathletes are born on Mars, though there are some who come from low-gravity environments.

Biathletes spend most of their time training, which means continually traveling about the planet on their own legs. Each biathlete has hidden stashes of supplies along commonly used routes, or a support team that places supplies at certain points. During the actual competition, it is violation of the rules to raid another biathlete's stores, so lack of supplies is the number one reason honest competitors fail to finish the race.

When not actively training or engaging in competition, biathletes act as guides for tourists who want to explore the Martian wilderness firsthand. Climbing tours are some of the most popular activities on Mars, even for native Martians, and Martian biathletes are uniquely qualified for the job. Even the best biathletes enjoy guiding tours since it gives them a chance to relax but still keep their skills sharp.

ATTRIBUTES ◇

AGI	0	APP	0	BUI	0	CRE	0	FIT	+2
INF	0	KNO	0	PER	0	PSY	0	WIL	+1
STR	+1	HEA	+1	STA	30	UD	4	AD	4

SKILLS ◇

Skill	Level	Attr.	Skill	Level	Attr.	Skill	Level	Attr.	Skill	Level	Attr.
Athletics	3	+2	First Aid	2	0	Mechanics	1	0	Survival	2	0
Earth Science	1	0	Land Navigation	2	0	Notice	1	0	Tinker	1	0

EQUIPMENT AND COST ◇

Typical Equipment:	Climbing gear, compact Mars tent, custom Mars suit
Salary:	50,000 to 2,000,000+ credits/year; paid by a sponsor or other means
Basic Costs:	21 Character Points, 30 Skill Points

ACTION CAMPAIGN USES ◇

With the conflict on Mars, the skills of a Martian biathlete are very useful as either a scout or infiltrator. In fact, many of the top biathletes formerly served with one of the national militaries. There are also innumerable emergencies that can occur during a climbing tour that allow the Martian biathlete to use their skills to aid others.

INTRIGUE CAMPAIGN USES ◇

Fame is a powerful tool when wielded properly, and a screen to hide all sorts of secrets. From being able to hire professional public relations help to gaining access to otherwise restricted areas, fame opens many doors. There is also the possibility that the biathlete's habits are less than acceptable socially, and thus require great secrecy.

POSSIBLE VARIATIONS ◇

If a biathlete is not already at the fore of their sport, they are either up-and-comers, retired and respected stars, or washed out has-beens. In each case, the challenges to playing this kind of character are numerous. For those craving action, a Player Character star biathlete can employee other Player Characters as bodyguards and assistants.

POSSIBLE SUBPLOTS ◇

Many successful athletes are also superstitious biathletes, engaging in good luck rituals and requiring their special charms to guarantee their continued success. The theft of one superstar biathlete's collection of lucky charms has the star upset and the management distraught, prior to the commencement of the big race. A lot of money is riding on a victory, and not just the athlete but also the sponsor's entire new product line depends on the recovery of the lost items.

GAME RESOURCES

THE STATES PARTIES TO THE PRESENT CONVENTION RECOGNIZING the desirability of determining by agreement uniform international rules regarding salvage operations,

NOTING that substantial developments have demonstrated the need to review the international rules presently contained in the International Convention on Salvage in Space, done at Geneva, 23 September 2059,

CONSCIOUS of the major contribution which efficient and timely salvage operations can make to the safety of vessels and other property in danger,

CONVINCED of the need to ensure that adequate incentives are available to persons who undertake salvage operations in respect of vessels and other property in danger,

HAVE AGREED as follows:

Chapter I — General provisions

Article 1 — Definitions

For the purpose of this Convention:

(a) Salvage operation means any act or activity undertaken to assist a vessel or any other property in danger in navigable space or in any other space environment whatsoever.

(b) Vessel means any ship or craft, or any structure capable of navigation.

(c) Property means any property not permanently and intentionally attached to the owner and includes freight at risk.

(d) Damage to the environment means substantial physical damage to human health or resources in open space or planetary proximity or areas adjacent thereto, caused by contamination, fire, explosion or similar major incidents.

(e) Payment means any reward, remuneration or compensation due under this Convention.

(f) Authority means the United Solar Nation's Space Navigation Authority.

(g) Chairperson means the Chairperson of the Authority.

Article 2 — Application of the Convention

This Convention shall apply whenever judicial or arbitral proceedings relating to matters with in this Convention are brought in a State Party.

Article 3 — Platforms

This Convention shall not apply to fixed or mobile platforms when such platforms or units are on location engaged in the exploration or exploitation production of mineral or organic resources, or conducting scientific research or exploration.

Article 4 — State-owned vessels

1. Without prejudice to article 5, this Convention shall not apply to warships or other non-commercial vessels owned or operated by a State and entitled, at the time of salvage operations, to sovereign immunity under generally recognized principles of international law unless that State decides otherwise.

2. Where a State Party decides to apply the Convention to its warships or other vessels described in paragraph 1, it shall notify the Chairperson thereof specifying the terms and conditions of such application.

Article 5 — Salvage operations controlled by public authorities

1. This Convention shall not affect any provisions of national law or any international convention relating to salvage operations by or under the control of public authorities.

2. Nevertheless, salvors carrying out such salvage operations shall be entitled to avail themselves of the rights and remedies provided for in this Convention in respect of salvage operations.

3. The extent to which a public authority under a duty to perform salvage operations may avail itself of the rights and remedies provided for in this Convention shall be determined the law of the State where such authority is situated.

Article 6 — Salvage contracts

1. This Convention shall apply to any salvage operations save to the extent that a contract otherwise provides expressly or by implication.

2. The master shall have the authority to conclude contracts for salvage operations on of the owner of the vessel. The master or the owner of the vessel shall have the authority to conclude such contracts on behalf of the owner of the property on board the vessel.

3. Nothing in this article shall affect the application of article 7 nor duties to prevent or minimize damage to the environment.

Article 7 — Annulment and modification of contracts

A contract or any terms thereof may be annulled or modified if:

(a) the contract has been entered into under undue influence or the influence of danger and terms are inequitable; or

(b) the payment under the contract is in an excessive degree too large or too small for the services actually rendered.

Chapter II — Performance of salvage operations

Article 8 — Duties of the salvor and of the owner and master

1. The salvor shall owe a duty to the owner of the vessel or other property in danger:

(a) to carry out the salvage operations with due care;

(b) in performing the duty specified in subparagraph (a), to exercise due care to prevent or minimize damage to the environment;

(c) whenever circumstances reasonably require, to seek assistance from other salvors; and

(d) to accept the intervention of other salvors when reasonably requested to do so by the owner or master of the vessel or other property in danger; provided however that the of his reward shall not be prejudiced should it be found that such a request was unreasonable.

2. The owner and master of the vessel or the owner of other property in danger shall owe a duty to the salvor:

(a) to co-operate fully with him during the course of the salvage operations;

(b) in so doing, to exercise due care to prevent or minimize damage to the environment;

(c) when the vessel or other property has been brought to a place of safety, to accept redelivery when reasonably requested by the salvor to do so.

Article 9 — Rights of Solar States

Nothing in this Convention shall affect the right of the State concerned to take measures in accordance with generally recognized principles of international law to protect the State's sphere of control or related interests from threat upon a spaceborne casualty or acts relating to such a casualty which may reasonably be expected to result in major harmful consequences, including the right of a State to give in relation to salvage operations.

Article 10 — Duty to render assistance

1. Every master is bound, so far as he can do so without serious danger to his vessel and persons thereon, to render assistance to any person in danger of being lost in space.

2. The States Parties shall adopt the measures necessary to enforce the duty set out in paragraph 1.

3. The owner of the vessel shall incur no liability for a breach of the duty of the master paragraph 1.

Article 11 — Co-operation

A State Party shall, whenever regulating or deciding upon matters relating to salvage operations such as admittance to ports of vessels in distress or the provision of facilities to salvors, take into account the need for co-operation between salvors, other interested and public authorities in order to ensure the efficient and successful performance of operations for the purpose of saving life or property in danger as well as preventing damage to the environment in general.

Chapter III — Rights of salvors

Article 12 — Conditions for reward

1. Salvage operations which have had a useful result give right to a reward.

2. Except as otherwise provided, no payment is due under this Convention if the salvage operations have had no useful result.

3. This chapter shall apply, notwithstanding that the salved vessel and the vessel performing the salvage operations belong to the same owner.

Article 13 — Criteria for fixing the reward

1. The reward shall be fixed with a view to encouraging salvage operations, taking into account the following criteria without regard to the order in which they are presented below:

(a) the salvaged value of the vessel and other property;

(b) the skill and efforts of the salvors in preventing or minimizing damage to the environment;

(c) the measure of success obtained by the salvor;

(d) the nature and degree of the danger;

(e) the skill and efforts of the salvors in salving the vessel, other property and life;

(f) the time used and expenses and losses incurred by the salvors;

(g) the risk of liability and other risks run by the salvors or their equipment;

(h) the promptness of the services rendered;

(i) the availability and use of vessels or other equipment intended for salvage operations;

(j) the state of readiness and efficiency of the salvor's equipment and the value thereof.

2. Payment of a reward fixed according to paragraph 1 shall be made by all of the vessel and other property interests in proportion to their respective salved values. However, a State may in its national law provide that the payment of a reward has to be made by one of interests, subject to a right of recourse of this interest against the other interests for their respective shares. Nothing in this article shall prevent any right of defence.

3. The rewards, exclusive of any interest and recoverable legal costs that may be payable thereon, shall not exceed the salved value of the vessel and other property.

Article 14 — Special compensation

1. If the salvor has carried out salvage operations in respect of a vessel which by itself or cargo threatened damage to the environment and has failed to earn a reward under article at least equivalent to the special compensation assessable in accordance with this article, he shall be entitled to special compensation from the owner of that vessel equivalent to his expenses as herein defined.

2. If, in the circumstances set out in paragraph 1, the salvor by his salvage operations has prevented or minimized damage to the environment, the special compensation payable by owner to the salvor under paragraph 1 may be increased up to a maximum of 30% of the expenses incurred by the salvor. However, the tribunal, if it deems it fair and just to do so bearing in mind the relevant criteria set out in article 13, paragraph 1, may increase such special compensation further, but in no event shall the total increase be more than 100% of the expenses incurred by the salvor.

3. Salvor's expenses for the purpose of paragraphs 1 and 2 means the out-of-pocket reasonably incurred by the salvor in the salvage operation and a fair rate for equipment and personnel actually and reasonably used in the salvage operation, taking into consideration criteria set out in article 13, paragraph 1 (h), (i) and (j).

4. The total special compensation under this article shall be paid only if and to the extent such compensation is greater than any reward recoverable by the salvor under article 13.

5. If the salvor has been negligent and has thereby failed to prevent or minimize damage the environment, he may be deprived of the whole or part of any special compensation due under this article.

6. Nothing in this article shall affect any right of recourse on the part of the owner of the vessel.

Article 15 — Apportionment between salvors

1. The apportionment of a reward under article 13 between salvors shall be made on the of the criteria contained in that article.

2. The apportionment between the owner, master and other persons in the service of each salving vessel shall be determined by the law of the flag of that vessel. If the salvage has been carried out from a vessel, the apportionment shall be determined by the law the contract between the salvor and his servants.

Article 16 — Salvage of persons

1. No remuneration is due from persons whose lives are saved, but nothing in this article shall affect the provisions of national law on this subject.

2. A salvor of human life, who has taken part in the services rendered on the occasion of accident giving rise to salvage, is entitled to a fair share of the payment awarded to the salvor for salving the vessel or other property or preventing or minimizing damage to the environment.

Article 17 — Services rendered under existing contracts

No payment is due under the provisions of this Convention unless the services rendered exceed what can be reasonably considered as due performance of a contract entered into before the danger arose.

Article 18 — The effect of salvor's misconduct

A salvor may be deprived of the whole or part of the payment due under this Convention to the extent that the salvage operations have become necessary or more difficult because of fault or neglect on his part or if the salvor has been guilty of fraud or other dishonest

Article 19 — Prohibition of salvage operations

Services rendered notwithstanding the express and reasonable prohibition of the owner or master of the vessel or the owner of any other property in danger which is not and has not been on board the vessel shall not give rise to payment under this Convention

Chapter IV — Claims and actions

Article 23 — Limitation of actions

1. Any action relating to payment under this Convention shall be time-barred if judicial or arbitral proceedings have not been instituted within a period of two years. The limitation period commences on the day on which the salvage operations are terminated.

2. Any action relating to payment under this Convention shall be time-barred if a derelict vessel or platform is salved after a ten year period commences on the date that the vessel or platform was reported lost.

3. The person against whom a claim is made may at any time during the running of the limitation period extend that period by a declaration to the claimant. This period may in like manner be further extended.

4. An action for indemnity by a person liable may be instituted even after the expiration of the limitation period provided for in the preceding paragraphs, if brought within the time allowed by the law of the State where proceedings are instituted.

Article 25 — State-owned cargoes

Unless the State owner consents, no provision of this Convention shall be used as a basis for the seizure, arrest or detention by any legal process of, nor for any proceedings in rem against, non-commercial cargoes owned by a State and entitled, at the time of the salvage operations, to sovereign immunity under generally recognized principles of international

Article 26 — Humanitarian cargoes

No provision of this Convention shall be used as a basis for the seizure, arrest or detention of humanitarian cargoes donated by a State, if such State has agreed to pay for salvage rendered in respect of such humanitarian cargoes.

Chapter V — Final clauses

Article 30 — Reservations

1. Any State may, at the time of signature, ratification, acceptance, approval or accession, reserve the right not to apply the provisions of this Convention:

(a) when the salvage operation takes place in the State's sphere of control and all vessels involved are of sphere of control navigation;

(b) when the salvage operations take place in the State's sphere of control and no vessel is involved;

(c) when all interested parties are nationals of that State;

(d) when the property involved is solar cultural property of archaeological historic interest and is situated in space.

Article 31 — Denunciation

1. This Convention may be denounced by any State Party at any time after the expiry of year from the date on which this Convention enters into force for that State.

Article 32 — Revision and amendment

1. A conference for the purpose of revising or amending this Convention may be by the Authority.

2. The Chairperson shall convene a conference of the States Parties to this for revising or amending the Convention, at the request of eight States Parties, or one of the States Parties, whichever is the higher figure.

Article 34 — Languages

This Convention is established in a single original in the Arabic, Chinese, English, French, Russian, Spanish, Venusian and Spacer's Runic languages, each text being equally authentic.

IN WITNESS WHEREOF the undersigned being duly authorized by their respective Governments for that purpose have signed this Convention.

DONE AT PYREA STATION this twenty-eighth day of November two thousand one hundred and eighty eight.

► BASIC SPACE GLOSSARY

The following list contains various space-related terms in common use among the space-faring societies of the 23rd century.

Aerobraking: a maneuver using friction with an atmosphere to decelerate a spacecraft.

Aeroshell: a heat shield used to protect a spacecraft during aerobraking or reentry.

Agora: the seat of the Jovian Confederacy's government. It is located in the Jovian capital of ElysÈe.

Airlock: a sealed chamber that can be independently pressurized, allowing movement to and from the vacuum of space.

Albedo: the reflecting power of a non-luminous body on a decimal scale of 0 to 1. A perfect reflector would have an albedo of 1, reflecting 100% of the light aimed at it.

Aperture: the diameter of the opening through which light passes in an optical instrument.

Aphelion: the farthest point that a body reaches in its orbit around the Sun.

Apoapsis: the farthest point that a body reaches on an orbit around any other body; the "generic" root of "aphelion" and "apogee."

Apogee: the highest point that a body reaches in its orbit around a planet.

Asteroid: small celestial body composed of metal, rock, ice, or any combination of the above.

Asteroid Belt: the region of space extending from approximately 2.2 to 3.3 AU from the Sun. Most of the asteroids orbit within this zone.

Astronomical Unit (AU): a unit of measure based on the distance from the Earth to the Sun. It is equal to $1,49 \times 10^8$ km and is commonly used for interplanetary flight.

Attitude: the orientation of a spacecraft to a given frame of reference.

Axis: an imaginary line around which a body rotates.

Barbecue Mode: a slow rolling maneuver that improves heat distribution on the skin of a spacecraft.

Bulkhead: a structural wall inside a spacecraft.

C Asteroid: carbonaceous asteroid, rich in organic matter, water-soluble salts, magnetite and clay minerals. They dominate the outer asteroid belt.

Caldera: a type of volcanic crater caused by the collapse of the ground after a powerful eruption; common on Venus and Io.

Central Earth Government and Administration: see CEGA.

CEGA: short for Central Earth Government and Administration. It is the ruling body that controls much of the Earth system.

Colony Cylinder: a huge, self-contained space station between 25 and 40 km in length, slowly rotating to generate one gee of gravity on the inside surface.

Cryogenic: very cold temperatures.

Deck: the floor level of a room, generally oriented toward the engines.

Delta V: change in the velocity of an object.

Deorbit Burn: a rocket thrust which reduces the orbital velocity of a body to lower its altitude, generally in preparation for reentry or landing.

Departure Velocity: the relative velocity of a spacecraft once it leaves a celestial body's gravitational field. Also known as hyperbolic velocity.

Deployment: releasing a payload or daughter craft to space.

Doppler Effect: the apparent change in the wavelength of light according to the motion of the body emitting it, in relation to the observer's position. It is used to calculate the velocity of a moving object.

Eccentricity: the measure of how well an orbit compares to a perfect circle; an eccentricity of 0 is a perfect circle, 1 is a parabolic orbit and greater than 1 is a hyperbolic orbit. Most planets have very low eccentricities, with Mercury and Pluto being the most extreme examples.

Ecliptic: the imaginary plane on which much of the solar system rotates; it is defined by the orbit of the Earth around the Sun.

Escape Velocity: the minimum velocity an object must reach to escape from the surface of a planetary body.

EVA: extra-vehicular activity, more commonly known as a space walk; going outside a craft in a space suit (called "going EVA").

Exo-Armors: large personal armors, standing around fifteen meters high and piloted from a cockpit usually located in their chest area.

Exo-Suits: also known as powered armors, or powered suits, they are smaller counterparts of the exo-armors. They are worn by their pilot and generally stand between two and three meters tall.

Floaters: secretive, giant "gas bag" creatures living in Jupiter's atmosphere. They are about as intelligent as a whale and can communicate with one another through electronic impulses.

Gee: A measure of acceleration, the gee (also noted as simply *g*) is equal to the pull exerted by the Earth at sea level. It is equal to 9.8 m/s2, though the rounded value of 10 m/s2 is used for most calculations.

Heliocentric: an orbit centered about the Sun.

Hohmann Transfer Orbit: an elliptical orbit where one end is tangent to the orbit of the point of departure and the other tangent to the orbit of the point of arrival. It is the lowest energy path from one point to another.

Hydrazine: a nitrogen-hydrogen compound that gives off energy when decomposing; it is used in very small (and thus simple) rocket motors.

Hypergolic Propellants: chemicals that ignite spontaneously on contact with each other; generally used in small maneuver engines or in weaponry (like the Wyvern's bazooka).

Hypersonic: a speed greater than five times the speed of sound.

Igloo: a temporary pressurized chamber (slang term).

Infrared: electromagnetic radiation with a wavelength longer than visible red light.

Integration: assembling payloads or components of a spacecraft in a desired configuration.

Kinetic Kill Cannons: a class of weapons cause damage by kinetic energy (movement). See Massdriver, Railgun.

KREEP: a rare and valuable type of lunar rock with a high content of potassium (chemical symbol: K), rare earth elements (REE) and phosphorus (P), all extremely useful elements.

Lagrange Points: five points in space located around two bodies that revolve around each other in nearly circular orbits; the gravitational forces of the two bodies combine with their motion and the motion of the points in space to provide regions of relative equilibrium at which other, smaller bodies (such as asteroids or colony cylinders) can "congregate" instead of orbiting independently — and, for colony cylinders, inconveniently — around the large bodies. Three points are located on the axis connecting the centers of the two large bodies: L1 is located between the two bodies, L2 is located "behind" the smaller body and L3 is located "behind" the larger body; these points are unstable and are largely useless except as curiosities. The L4 and L5 points, however, are stable enough to be useful. They are located on the orbit of the smaller of the two large bodies and are found 60 degrees "ahead" (L4) and 60 degrees "behind" (L5).

Laser: acronym for Light Amplification by Stimulated Emission of Radiation, a laser is a beam of coherent light, used for long range communication or to superheat and destroy a target.

LEO: short for Low Earth Orbit, a 300- to 600-kilometer radius, nearly circular orbit with a period of about ninety minutes for Earth.

LH: liquid hydrogen; it's a cryogenic fluid which must be kept at extremely low temperatures.

Linear Frame: the main control element of an exo-armor. It looks like an industrial exo-skeleton and completely supports the pilot, reproducing his every movement.

LOX: liquid oxygen; it's a cryogenic fluid which must be kept at very low temperatures.

Magnetic Sail (MagSails): a thin ring-like device that generates a magnetic field that can be pushed by the solar wind and the magnetic field of planets. It is a somewhat slow propulsion system, but it requires no propellant and is thus very economic. Magnetic sails have low field density but occupy a large volume of space (in excess of 60 km for even the smallest ships).

Maser: a beam of microwave radiation, used as a detection device or (more rarely) as a weapon.

Massdriver: a weapon that uses a series of magnetic rings to fire a hail of small shells.

Missiles: self-propelled, self-guided projectiles, using sophisticated guidance computers and laser targeting technology.

M-Pods: tiny free flying spacecraft used to move objects around (slang term).

Nomads: colloquial term for groups of people that live on asteroids, outside of mainstream human society.

Occultation: the concealment of one celestial body by another.

O'Neill Island: a type of colony cylinder that uses glass panels and mirrors to direct sunlight inside. Island Type I is a sphere with agricultural rings attached, while both Island Types II and III are large cylinders with reflective mirrors.

Orbit: the path traced by a celestial body (natural or artificial).

Particle Cannon: also known as beam cannon, it is a magnetic accelerator designed to shoot ions instead of a solid slug. They cause damage through a combination of kinetic energy, heat and induced electrical charge.

Periapsis: the closest point that a body reaches on an orbit around any other body; the "generic" root of "perihelion" and "perigee."

Perigee: the lowest point that a body reaches in its orbit around a planet.

Perihelion: the closest point that a body reaches in its orbit around the Sun.

Plasma: very hot gaseous mix of high-energy electrons and ions moving freely about.

Plasma Combustion Chamber (PCC): one of the most common types of space propulsion systems in use. Using an inert gas or liquid as reaction mass (most often hydrogen or water), the PCC enables spacecraft to achieve great acceleration for extended periods, reducing travel times to mere weeks and, sometimes, mere days.

Plasma Lance: a compressed-gas cylinder with an ionizer ejector system at one end. Powerful current transforms the gas into a giant plasma flame that can be used as a cutting weapon.

Railgun: a weapon that magnetically accelerates a single projectile via twin rails along the length of the barrel.

Regolith: loose top layer of soil found on airless celestial bodies; it is made up of crushed rock, dust and meteor debris.

Rem: a unit of measure for radiation.

S Asteroid: stony asteroid, rich in silicates of iron and magnesium, feldspar, iron-nickel alloy and iron sulfide.

Screen Generator: a device that protects the vehicle or space suit on which it is mounted by either absorbing or deflecting the radiation striking it.

Shield Volcano: volcano with a large base and gentle slopes created by repeated lava flow; the famous Mont Olympus on Mars is the largest one in the Solar System.

Sidereal Period: the revolution period of a satellite around its primary as measured against the nearly fixed background of stars. In the case of planet Earth, it is equal to one year.

Skyhook: a more feasible kind of "space elevator" that allows cargo to be hoisted up into orbit. It consists of a long tether extending from a low orbit station down into the upper atmosphere and up into space. Hypersonic suborbital planes can match velocities with the lower end of the tether to hook up their cargo rather than spend the energy to go up to a full orbit.

Snowball: slang term for water ice-rich bodies such as comet cores.

Sol: one Martian day, equal to 24.6 Earth hours.

SolaPol: the law-enforcement agency of the United Space Nations.

Solar Sail: an extremely thin, highly reflective sail that is pushed by light beams (either solar or laser-generated). It is a slow propulsion system, but it requires no propellant and is thus very economic. Solar sails are extremely fragile and occupy a large area of space (several square kilometers for even the smaller ships).

Solar Wind: the sleet of charged plasma from the Sun that travels outward into the solar system. It is used to drive MagSails.

Specific Impulse: a measure of the performance of rocket engines; it is the number of seconds an engine will supply one kilogram of thrust on one kilogram of fuel. The higher the number, the more efficient the engine is. It is often abbreviated as *Isp*.

Solar Power Satellite (SPS): these are used to gather sunlight and convert it to electrical power ready to be beamed to a nearby world or colony.

SSTO: short for "single stage to orbit" — a spacecraft that does not need to discard boosters or other rocket stages to reach orbit.

Terminator: the boundary between the illuminated ("day") and dark ("night") portions of a planet or satellite.

Transit: the apparent passage of a small celestial body across the face of a larger one.

Ultraviolet: electromagnetic radiation with a wavelength shorter than visible violet light.

United Space Nations (USN): an advisory council, the USN is the successor of the 20th century's United Nations.

Van Allen Belts: radiation zones of charged particles trapped in powerful magnetic field lines.

Venusian Bank: a powerful economic corporation, based on Venus.

Vivarium Colony: a type of colony cylinder that is closed and thickly protected against radiation, relying on a "sunline" running along its axis to provide illumination. Mostly used by the Jovian Confederation.